I0613257

The Case of the Vanishing Girls

Wildcat Crew 1

K.C. Sprayberry

ALL RIGHTS RESERVED

No part of this book may be reproduced or transmitted in any form or by any means, electronic or mechanical, including photocopying, recording, or by any information storage and retrieval system, without permission in writing from the author, except in the case of brief quotations embodied in reviews.

Publisher's Note:

This is a work of fiction. All names, characters, places, and events are the work of the author's imagination.

Any resemblance to real persons, places, or events is coincidental.

Solstice Publishing - www.solsticepublishing.com

Copyright 2017 K.C. Sprayberry

Chapter One

The moon hung low on a dark California night. June could be a mix of summer's warmth with just enough of the coolness left over from spring to force the native Californians to retreat to their homes and huddle beneath blankets.

Fools they were, and The Mastermind would be the one to remind them of their folly. For he was the one who would wake them up from their quiet, peaceful lives and thrust them into the terror of his making. No one would rest easily until he had sated his hunger.

He crept along a quiet street. Homes were lit up. Images of families having an ordinary evening played through his mind. They had no idea of what he was about to unleash on them. His plan was very simple—no one had noticed his first attempt at fame a mere four years ago, because of the Manson Family's rampage.

They will now. No one will ever ignore me again.

At one house, he stopped near an open window. The voices within rose in what appeared to be anger; he smiled. This type of confrontation was what filled his heart with joy.

"You never want me to have any fun," a girl cried out in frustration.

He knew that voice, had heard it on many occasions, but putting a name to the near childish timbre was almost impossible. Creeping around a hydrangea bush, he pressed against the outer wall and glanced sideways. No one could see him here. The overgrown bush was almost a tree and the streetlights didn't cast their brightness this far.

"Your father and I have told you time after time that we will not let you wear the disgusting fashions girls have adopted these days," an older woman said. "You have to accept our decision, Suzie. We are your parents. You can do nothing without our permission until you are twenty-one."

"Why? Because of what happened? Because you think by making me into some kind of dummy living in the past will stop me from leaving?"

"Because I will not tolerate the looseness and disrespect of your generation."

"Good grief, Mother," Suzie said— he finally remembered her name, Suzie Calderone, a complete loser. "The age of legal consent is eighteen, and I am eighteen.

You can't stop me from doing what I want with my life."

"I beg your pardon, young lady," a man said. "Eighteen most certainly is not the age of legal consent. We've had this discussion before; all you children got back in 1971 was the right to vote. No one has ever passed a law to make eighteen the legal age."

"OHHHHHHH!" Suzie exclaimed in total exasperation. "Boys were sent to Vietnam to die at eighteen. We can vote at eighteen. We can get our own driver's license and move into our own home at eighteen. What more do we need for our parents to understand that we are adults? Get with the times, Mom and Dad. This isn't the fifties. It's nineteen-seventy-three! The world has changed!"

"Apologize to your mother immediately," Dad said. "I will not tolerate your insolence another minute."

"Goodbye!" Suzie yelled. "I won't apologize to the people who have destroyed my whole life."

A few minutes later, a door slammed. The man behind the shrubbery inched out, making sure that no one could see him. She was walking away at high speed. He smiled. His first target was making this so easy.

***

The foothills above Monrovia retained some of the glow from the moon but not enough for her to escape his excellent tracking skills. A smile revealed his white teeth and he quickly closed his lips. No one could catch him this night. He'd succeed now, just as he'd done a few years ago.

He'd tricked the police into believing he hadn't remembered the night his whole family was murdered, even with his clothing soaked in their blood. At the time, he'd thought for certain they would see through his pathetic excuses, but the pigs had lapped up his lies and treated him like a king.

No one will ever figure out it's me. I'll get away with this just like I got away with killing my family for being such losers. Damn Charlie Manson and his followers for ruining my great move. Everyone talked about them instead of me.

Timing was everything, as he'd learned the hard way. A mere ten days after his glorious act, people stopped talking about a horrendous crime in Monrovia and concentrated on the events taking place in Beverly Hills.

I can't wait any longer. I have to do this again. The world will fear me. I won't stop until there is no one left that doesn't believe I am the king of killing.

He was fed by an insatiable thirst to feel life seeping out of a body, but not just one life at a time. He also had to wait until the right day. For his scheme to be perfect, he would have to capture and contain a total of seven people, four men and three women—seven was the magic number. It was the same number of people the Manson Family had killed over two days. The Mastermind, however, would be better than that loser. His spree would last a single night of unmitigated horror. His only problem was that being stuck in boring old Monrovia he had no chance of capturing anyone famous.

He was young. He had time. But he hated the feeling of being cheated out of fame. No one had yet to hear of the actions of The Mastermind, but they would. He would gain more notice than the Manson Family or any other fruitcake that wasn't good enough to remain free while the pigs ran around trying to find *him*.

They'll never think it's me. He snickered, a low and slithering sound, reminiscent of the coyotes that occasionally crept out of the foothills. *They already decided I could never do something so awful.*

His target tonight was a snitch. She was trouble waiting to happen. Word of her transgression had reached him by chance. If he hadn't decided to eat in the cafeteria earlier today, he wouldn't have known that she'd been bragging about seeing him after he'd committed a "victimless" crime.

He'd been trying to get some extra cash, to make up for the money his loser uncle was withholding from him. His parents' estate was his to use as he pleased but creepy old Uncle Andy had said The Mastermind couldn't have a penny until after he graduated high school, and only then if he went to college. So what if he'd been ripping off some stupid neighbors with a bunch of expensive stuff in their houses? That little brat wouldn't tell anyone that she saw him. He'd make sure of that.

She was his first problem. There were more, but they could wait. He would get them eventually.

I'll get that old man. Just wait until no one is looking, when the cops are off searching for some transient to blame the latest round of grisly murders on. Then I'll take out my miserly uncle and no one will suspect me.

He grinned when his target hurried toward the canyon. Everyone thought she was a goody-goody, but he knew better. She'd given him the perfect hiding place to keep her and the others he would capture up here, until he could begin his own reign of terror.

***

Suzie hated her life. No one at Monrovia High School paid much attention to her. She was smart but afraid to show anyone that. Instead, she skated along in the middle of the class, rarely participating in discussions or extra-curricular activities. She'd graduate next week, six days before the summer solstice. While the rest of the seniors were partying on the beach on the longest day of the year, she'd be sneaking out of town.

Her master plan was to get to New York and become a runway model. That she was a mere five-foot, four-inches didn't deter her. Nor did her pudginess put her off. She was going to be the premier runway model of Fifth Avenue.

What had her worried now was the fight with her parents. They were so old-fashioned and stupid if she thought about their behavior enough. Imagine, forcing her to look like she was stuck in the fifties and be made the butt of a million awful jokes in school. Their attitude had cost her any chance of friends, not that she wanted the shallow fools around here as friends.

What was even worse was that they hadn't always lived like this. After her brother and sister messed up, her parents had vanished from their luxury home in Beverly Hills and remade their lives, even going so far as to change their last name. She missed Christine and George. They were fun to have around, but now that she was without them, Suzie had plans of her own and no one would stop her.

Tension ripped through her. She could feel a headache coming on. That always happened after an argument with her parents. They would probably expect her to come back home and pound on the door until the whole neighborhood was watching and listening before they dragged her back into the house for another round of humiliation.

That won't happen tonight. I won't go back until after school tomorrow. Let them feel my pain for once.

She itched to use her secret stash. Pulling it out here, on the street, was really stupid. Suzie wasn't dumb by any means, but her hands were shaking and her whole body ached for a few puffs on a joint. The only thing about her preferred method of escaping her life was that it was illegal.

I'm just going to relax.

She touched the baggie in a pocket of her shorts—not the currently popular mini-shorts, but a pair that barely skimmed her knees. Her parents were the reason she didn't have any clothes that were fun and in style. It was their stupid rules that had her squirming whenever she had to put on something that looked like it had been in someone's attic for the last twenty years. They didn't let her do anything fun. Their antiquated ideas had made her high school years a living hell.

"This stuff isn't really bad for people." She glanced in all directions, to make sure no one was around. "It just makes me feel good."

If her parents ever knew she came up to the canyon to smoke joints, they would literally kill her. Their constant rules and stupid ways of making her different from everyone else had put a lot of stress on her. Suzie had to find a way to relax or she would explode all over everyone.

Quiet footsteps behind her as she stepped off the road and into the brushy canyon had her hurrying to her private spot. No one knew about this place that she was aware of. She hadn't known about it until she stumbled upon it a few months ago, after a similar argument with her parents. Two stories high, it had a huge porch with columns supporting a domed skylit area in front of the doors. The paint was peeling away, if not completely gone in places. The house itself appeared to have been uncared for many, many years. Inside, there was a sensation of evil, of horrific acts committed there but she ignored that because there was a wonderful hiding place in a small basement where she could watch the moon on nights like this while she got high to forget how bad she felt.

I'll stay here all night. She picked her way across the cracked tile to a staircase near the rear of the building.

Getting down the stairs was difficult. They were rotting away and she'd forgotten a flashlight. Yet, she managed and felt her way over to a spot far from where anyone might find her on the chance that noise earlier meant a person had noticed her walking up this way.

Nobody will know I'm here.

Suzie squatted onto a pile of discarded junk in a room deep within the building. She pulled out a joint and a Bic lighter. Seconds later, she reclined against a wall and drew the smoke into her lungs. After blowing that out, she inhaled again.

The tension released. She floated on a cloud of smoke and bliss that no one would have ever expected of her. It was only when a flashlight illuminated her face that she realized someone was with her.

"Who is that?"

She dropped the still burning joint and smashed it with her sneaker, regretting wasting nearly half. The light blinded her from seeing if it was another pot smoker or the cops.

I'm so busted.

All she could hear was heavy breathing.

"Who are you?"

The person behind the light didn't speak. Suzie stumbled to her feet and shaded her eyes with an arm. She could barely make out the outline of a man. It had to be a man. He was tall, probably over six feet, and he was just standing there, watching her.

"Why...?"

Her voice took on a note of panic. She was pretty high, even though she'd only taken two hits. The pot she'd bought from her source was supposed to be the best grade available. She figured that was why she was having so much trouble talking to the intruder.

"You're the first."

His voice was familiar. Suzie backed away in fear. She knew who this was. Everyone thought he was such a great guy, a fabulous athlete, and so pathetic after... after...

"What do you want?"

Her fear rose until her heart was beating at thundering levels when he approached her. Suzie tried to push around him but he was so much stronger than she was. She felt the flashlight crash against her head.

She fell forward and struggled to rise. She could feel a man grabbing her but then her eyes fluttered shut.

***

He smiled and wrapped ropes around her arms, tying her to a post near where she'd been smoking.

She started to come around, moaning.

"There will be others," he said, his voice smug, gloating. "You won't be alone long."

Chapter Two

Marnie Wildwood swung her purse over a shoulder and locked her hot red Camaro. The car was an early graduation gift from her parents—to reward her for being an honor graduate. Initially, she'd wanted to go to Stanford, but in the last week, she and her close friends had decided to remain in the area and attend Citrus Community College in nearby Azusa. They'd all figured that they would have an easier time setting up their new business while still attending school and getting a degree. Their only problem lay in the fact that they needed a serious case to attract potential clients to their doors.

A short breeze blew her waist-length auburn hair across her face. Marnie shoved it back. Taller than most girls her age, she was slender with hazel eyes. At times, people thought she could be a model but she was happiest figuring out mysteries and taking pictures of unusual sights.

Her only plans today were to enjoy the rest of the last week of high school and figure out if there were any new mysteries to solve.

Marnie's destination was a place she and her crew had taken over long ago—the school's friendship circle, a central location that gave them the opportunity to watch everyone coming and going while also having the chance to talk without interruption.

"Hey, Marnie!" Les—never call her Leslie—Johnson waved and ran toward Marnie. "Wait for me."

Marnie waved back and grinned at Les. Les was petite with a cap of strawberry blonde curls framing a heart-shaped face. Her bright blue eyes often danced with excitement and she adored any outdoors activity.

There was part of the problem Marnie faced. She, Les, Tish Ramone, and Garth Michaelson were the Wildcat Crew. They were sort of investigators, of the funniest kind, in Marnie's opinion. All of them were avid readers and adored cats, each owning at least one feline. What gave them the reputation of being sort of investigators were their cases. Unlike Nancy Drew or the Hardy Boys, they didn't stumble onto earthshaking mysteries where they had to seek out clues for days on end or confront conspirators who might cause horrible damage to their area. In fact, all four of them yearned for a case as interesting as these fictional characters solved with regularity.

Nancy Drew and Frank and Joe Hardy have never had to put up with the kind of cases we're called on to solve.

The Wildcat Crew was most famous for uncovering the fact that Mr. Green's roses were turning yellow because Billy Martin was peeing on them. Once that came to light, Billy confessed that he was doing that because he wanted his grandmother's roses to win the blue ribbon at the county fair—an honor Mr. Green had taken for decades.

Their next case was even sillier—discovering who was beating up Mrs. Smith's mailbox with a ball bat. Since she was well known for her hostile attitude, the suspect list was quite long, but it didn't take long for the quartet to uncover the fact that Mary Ellen Masters, a local softball star, had been buying new bats at least three times a week. Mary Ellen confessed to Mrs. Smith and the police that the act was done because Mrs. Smith had herself committed the crime of squirting Mary Ellen's Persian cat, Jethro, with a garden hose several times.

No charges were filed in those cases or our last one. Marnie shook her head in dismay. *When are we going to get a serious case? How can I become a female private investigator if no one will let us solve something important?*

Their third major case, the one she worried might forever doom them to the prank category, was figuring out how all the trash cans in Library Park ended up on top of the library. Not only that, but they were placed in a pattern that resembled a star. It had taken the Wildcat Crew a week to figure out the football team had played a prank. They were now on probation. If they did anything wrong before school ended next Wednesday, they would all be working with the janitors, cleaning up the buildings while everyone else was headed for the beach.

Except Terry Jacobson.

Marnie frowned. She had never liked him, even though everyone else felt sorry for the quarterback.

He always gets away with everything. Why can't anyone else see what a real creep he is?

"Did you hear?" Les stopped beside Marnie.

"Hear what?" Marnie asked.

Her interest was definitely piqued. Maybe Les had word of a case in the making, one they could investigate and solve before the police were involved.

"Suzie Calderone is missing," Les said with a dramatic flair. "She took off after arguing with her parents last night and hasn't been seen since."

The first thing that struck Marnie was that Suzie had argued with her parents. Suzie was the meekest person in the universe. She wouldn't mash a flea, in case someone thought she was murdering it. The second thing was that Suzie had taken off. She didn't have any close friends and made the expression "keeps to herself" seem tame.

"Are you sure she isn't just hanging around in the cafeteria?" Marnie asked. "I just can't believe that Suzie would take off."

"Yeah, that does seem really strange." Les glanced toward the area where the cafeteria was. "Who eats in there? It's cramped and hot all the time. I'd rather get food from a roach coach."

No one knew the real reason mobile lunch wagons were named "roach coach," but it was enough to keep everyone from ordering anything that wasn't a drink or prewrapped. A few kids claimed they knew people who had gotten ill after eating from one of those places, but it was always a friend of the mother of a great aunt, or some other really strange relationship.

"True." Marnie caught a glimpse of Tish and Garth headed their way. "Here comes the rest of the team. Maybe they have a clue."

Tish's shoulder-length red hair was a tangle of waves around her well-sculpted face. Green eyes peered out from lush lashes, made that way from an overuse of mascara. Marnie's height, Tish excelled in track and field and swimming, winning honors in both sports this year.

Tall and lanky, his six foot, three-inch frame had Garth towering over most of their class, even some of the basketball players. He had been friends with all three girls since kindergarten. His black hair was just below his ears, and he sported the thick sideburns that had recently become fashionable. Black eyes sparkled with repressed laughter. He loved playing pranks when they weren't solving mysteries, and exploring the desert.

Garth and Tish stopped in front of Marnie and Les.

"Hear about Suzie?" Tish asked.

"Yeah." Les nodded. "What do you know?"

"She was seen on Canyon Road last night," Garth said. "Went up into the hills but never came back down. That was near midnight."

"How do you know that?" Les asked. "It wasn't on the news." She smacked her forehead. "Oh, your dad. Right?"

"Yup." Garth nodded. "He was talking to the police as I left this morning. They want the DA up there, to keep him involved from the onset. Can I help it if I found the conversation fascinating?"

Marnie's brain kicked into overdrive. Her dad got a call to a potential crime scene at six this morning. That was about the time most teens were getting up, to be at the bus stop before seven. Suzie lived on the south end of town, meaning her parents would have discovered she wasn't in the house about that time.

Why didn't Dad tell me it was a missing person case?

Her dad was an investigator with the Monrovia Police Department. He'd discouraged Marnie from going to college to be a police officer, even though women officers were being allowed to patrol and become detectives now. His reasons made a lot of sense to her, but she still wanted to check out crimes, solve them, and be an important part of the whole process.

"How did she get from the south side of town up to Canyon Road?" Les asked. "I can't see Suzie walking all that way."

"True." Marnie glanced around when the first bell rang. "Put your thinking caps on but don't let this interfere with our classes. There's still five days before we graduate."

"You're not going to believe the weirdest part," Garth said. "There was a note stuck on a telephone pole at the top of Canyon Road."

"What did it say?" Tish asked.

"'She's mine,'" he said. "And there was an 'H' and an 'S' intertwined on the bottom, dripping and red, like you know…"

His voice trailed off. Marnie shuddered. Four years ago, everyone in the Los Angeles area had lived in horrific fear of the Manson Family. Those criminals had been in prison since 1971, although their death sentences had been reduced to life in prison after the state overturned the death penalty.

It can't be someone using "Helter Skelter." No way. That is just too creepy.

After some serious thinking, she latched onto another murder that was just as gruesome but still unsolved. This one had happened right here in Monrovia, a mere ten days before the Manson murders.

Terry Jacobson. His whole family was killed on the last day of July.

Marnie trailed after her friends, lost in thought about a case that still frustrated her dad.

Is there a connection between then and now?

Chapter Three

Marnie and the rest of Wildcat Crew gathered in the friendship circle once school ended for the day. None of them had jobs, as their parents wanted them to concentrate on their studies. Homework was light to nonexistent since the teachers were putting together the end of year report cards. Their afternoon was free and Marnie had the perfect thing for them to do.

"Garth, you and Les go to Suzie's house," she said. "See if you can ask her parents a few questions. Maybe you can get to the bottom of how she got from the south side to Canyon Road."

That was the biggest part of this mystery. Monrovia wasn't as big as some cities in the Los Angeles basin, but it was a good ten to fifteen-mile walk from where Suzie lived to Canyon Road. Someone would have noticed a teen out that late at night.

"Gotcha." Garth grabbed Les' hand and they took off.

"What are we doing?" Tish asked.

"We are going to bug my dad," Marnie said, wrinkling her nose. "I'm going to get him to admit that those weird letters on the bottom of that note do not mean someone else is using the Helter Skelter thing to make everyone crazy again."

"Great idea."

The girls rushed to Marnie's Camaro and were soon on their way to the Monrovia Police Station. While she was sure her dad would be at the crime scene, he'd probably get upset if she showed up asking questions.

The drive to the Library Park area was quiet. Marnie's thoughts were swirling around.

None of this makes sense. Nobody in their right mind would ever use that logo on their criminal act. Would they?

"This is really strange," Tish said. "I mean, who would use an "H" and an "S" on a note? It just doesn't make sense. Why would someone want to scare everyone and put the cops on high alert?"

"No clue."

Once they were at the station, Marnie and Tish discovered their not-so-sparkling reputation as amateur detectives had been tarnished beyond redemption. Her dad was out, which she took to mean he was at the crime scene. Exactly where that scene was had her wondering; the moment she asked if he was at Suzie's house, all the officers had burst into laughter but they quickly found other things to do when she kept asking to talk to him.

"That was a total loss." Tish glared at the station once they were on the sidewalk. "Those guys are total jerks."

"Not usually," Marnie said, but her mind on what she considered their current case. "I did pick up on one thing."

"What's that?" Tish had a puzzled expression on her face.

"My dad isn't at Suzie's house," Marnie said. "And since they have no idea where she is, he's not there either."

"True." Tish shook her head. "Where would he be?"

A glance toward City Hall gave Marnie an idea. She recognized the dark colored four door sedan parked in front of the building. Her dad wasn't at a crime scene. It appeared he was with the mayor and city council.

"What are you thinking?" Tish asked.

"The guys at the station said my dad was at the crime scene." Marnie pointed at City Hall. "How could Suzie have gotten in there?"

Tish glanced in that direction. Her mouth fell open. She stared at Marnie in shock.

"What is going on?" Tish asked. "Why did they lie to you?"

"I have no idea, but I'm about to find out."

They hurried over to Myrtle Avenue and waited for traffic to clear. School would close for the summer soon. More cars than usual clogged the two-lane street. On-street parking made things worse, with drivers waiting for a spot or trying to back out. Several of the popular shops with the latest fashions sported signs offering unreal prices. A mere ten dollars for a bikini. Matching mini shorts with a body slimming tank top for only nine-ninety-five. Sandals were being advertised for three dollars! Summer bargains were everywhere!

No one appeared to be worried that one teenager had vanished overnight.

It's like no one cares that Suzie is missing.

"Street's clear." Tish grabbed Marnie's hand. "Let's go before the light changes."

They ran across the street and hurried into City Hall. Marnie walked toward the mayor's office as if she belonged in the building and had business to discuss. This tactic had worked for her in the past, when she was checking out information.

"Just a minute." An officer stepped in front of the girls right before they reached the mayor's office. "You can't come in here today."

"Why?" Tish asked.

"There's a closed session of the council." He smirked at them. "Get on home, girls. Nothing for you here. We'll call you the next time someone stacks trash cans on the library's roof."

"I'm here to see my dad." Marnie leaned past him. "Dad? We need to talk."

She raised her voice, to be certain he got the message. A couple of minutes later, a door further down the hallway opened and her dad hurried toward them.

"I have this, officer," Dad said. "Return to your post."

He turned to the girls with a furious expression. Marnie stepped back. She'd never seen him so angry.

"You will not get involved," Dad said. "I already know what you're thinking and you will not get involved in this case."

"Dad," she said. "Suzie is one of our classmates and really quiet. She's the last person who would run away from home."

"Yes, she's a classmate," he said, "but you don't really know her." One of his eyebrows shot up. "Do you?"

"Sort of," Tish said. "She's not very friendly with anyone. More people would like her if she wasn't always so angry."

"Exactly," he said. "She's angry all the time. Back off. This is probably a situation where we'll find Suzie on a bus headed for New York. Her parents indicated that's where she wanted to go to college."

"Why would she take off five days before graduation?" Marnie asked. "She won't be able to get into college without her diploma." She tilted her head to the side and stare at him seriously. "What about that note?"

"It's not connected. Don't even think about some silly note a kid probably put on the phone pole to create a fuss as being part of this. Marnie, please, go home. Lock the door once you're inside," Dad said. "Leave this one to me."

The girls had run into his exasperated attitude before, when they wanted information on the ball bat case. Marnie glanced at Tish. Both nodded.

"Later, Dad." Marnie kissed his cheek and left.

That scene bothered Marnie all the way back to the high school. There were absolutely no clues as to why someone would want to associate a message with such a horrible event. They didn't even know for certain the note had anything to do with Suzie's disappearance. All they really knew was that Suzie had a fight with her parents and took off.

No real surprise there. Her parents have made her dress like she's living in the fifties. That's been hard on her.

Marnie pulled into the parking lot and stopped by Tish's El Camino.

"Do we need snacks?" she asked.

"Yeah." Marnie nodded. "Mom's at a class today. Dad will probably be stuck at work until late. Burger place up the street?"

"Yummy." Tish grinned. "Meet you there."

Marnie made sure her friend was in her car and starting the engine before heading to the burger shack a block north. This place was absolutely fabulous and luckily, there was no one in the parking lot. After making sure she had enough money to cover burgers for four starving teens, she dashed through the door. The sound of a car pulling into the lot had her glancing over her shoulder, thinking that Tish got here fast.

"Hey, Marnie," Officer James Hamilton called. "Your dad asked you to bring enough for him too. He's getting a dinner break in about forty minutes."

"Okay, got it." She grabbed her wallet and made sure the twenty she always shoved into a secret pocket was still there. "Great. We can have enough fries too."

She headed for the counter and took a cursory glance at the menu.

"Ten triple burgers with five large fries," Marnie said. "And four vanilla shakes."

The clerk rang up the order and Marnie paid.

"It'll take about twenty minutes," the clerk said.

"No problem," Marnie said. "Can I have some containers to get all the toppings? I don't know who wants what on their burgers."

"Sure." She pulled out a stack of Styrofoam burger containers. "Sounds like you're having a party."

"Nah, just my friends and my dad."

Marnie walked slowly over to the counter where the toppings were. She didn't need to worry about the condiments. There were enough of those at home. Her mind wandered to the case she wanted to solve, and her dad sending an officer to ask her to order dinner for him. That was really weird that the officer knew where she was.

Maybe Dad had someone follow us here. We weren't paying attention. Tish and I were really quiet. I was thinking all the way back.

Tish showed up as Marnie was piling toppings into the container. She helped and Marnie laughed when they cleaned out the pickles.

"Well, everybody loves pickles," Tish said. "Can't have too many."

"You have that right." Marnie nodded at one of the containers. "Grab all the onions too. We might as well compete with Garth for the bad breath."

"On it." Tish worked on stuffing onions into a container.

"Hey, Marnie, order's up."

"Be right there." Marnie closed the lid on the lettuce. "I'll get a bag for this stuff."

She went to the counter and got a bag for Tish before balancing the bags of steaming food and a drink container with the shakes. After the girls set the food in Marnie's car, Tish got in her El Camino.

"Meet you at your place." Tish took off almost too fast.

Her back end swayed from side to side as she made the turn. Marnie drove a whole lot slower. She didn't want to spill the food all over her carpeting. It would take forever to get out.

Twenty minutes later, Tish and Marnie were carrying the food into the house. Garth and Les arrived in their vehicles and gave them a hand.

"Your dad sent an officer to tell us where you were," Garth said. "He said it was a good idea for us to leave the Calderones house right away."

"Yeah." Les rolled her eyes. "Suzie's parents are complete jerks."

"Really?" Marnie asked. "I've never met them. What did they say?"

"We'll talk while we're eating," Garth said. "I don't want my fries to get cold."

Once the teens were set up at the kitchen table, with Marnie putting her dad's food in the oven so it stayed warm, they began eating.

"It was so weird at Suzie's house," Les said around munching on her pickle and onion-laden burger. "Her parents acted like she broke the law or something. They couldn't stop saying what an awful person she is."

"Yeah." Garth nodded, mashing his burger; the monster high stack of meat, cheese, and double handfuls of each topping was too much to fit into his mouth. "What's with them anyway? Suzie took off and they don't seem to care if she ever comes back."

Marnie opened her mouth to respond but Dad came through the door.

"In the oven?" he asked.

"Yup," she said. "Do you have enough coffee?"

"Right here." He held up a huge Styrofoam cup. "Mind if I sit in on this discussion?"

This was a first, but she was willing if her friends were. Marnie glanced at them and they nodded.

"Sure."

"Okay, here's the set-up." Dad sat down and began putting toppings on his burgers. "You kids have official permission to help this time."

All four teens cheered.

"But there are limitations," he said, mashing his burger down. "By the way, nice meal. Just what I wanted. Thanks."

"You're welcome," Marnie said. "What's the limitation?"

"All you can do is talk to one suspect, but you can't let him know he's a suspect."

"Why?" Tish asked, slurping down some shake.

"Because we think he'll respond better to someone his own age."

Marnie frowned. She hadn't thought she'd be asked to do the police department's job when it came to interviewing a potential suspect.

"What if he did do it and says we entrapped him?" Garth asked.

"You won't do that," Dad said. "Just talk to this person as if all of you were talking about the problem. Find out what he knows, and if there's anything her parents might be holding back."

"Who is it?" Tish asked.

"Brad Montgomery," he said. "Someone saw him running down Canyon Road around midnight. His parents swear that he was in bed but the witness was very adamant."

"Who is the witness?" Marnie asked.

"Terry Jacobson," Dad said. "He was outside putting the trash in the can. That's why he saw Brad."

"Really?" Tish asked. "I thought he lived a couple of blocks from the high school."

"His uncle moved them into the house up here a few months back," Dad said. "Personally, I would never make a child live in a home where his family was murdered, but it appears that's where Terry wants to be."

Marnie ate her food and concentrated on the convenience of Terry seeing Brad running along Canyon Road last night. Brad was a science geek with greasy hair, glasses always in need of a cleaning, and, until recently, a terminal case of acne. Exercise and Brad were allergic to each other.

Why do I think Terry was the one running down Canyon Road last night and not Brad?

But she knew she had to talk to Brad before blowing off his possible connection to Suzie's disappearance. Marnie might feel the tip was bad but she had to check it out.

Chapter Four

Marnie waved goodbye to her friends before closing and locking the kitchen door. Mom wouldn't be home for another couple of hours. The courses she was taking at Citrus College a few towns over didn't end until nine. After all these years, she wanted the teaching degree she'd given up on when she got pregnant with Marnie. Dad had gone back to the police station, to check in with the desk sergeant, and Marnie was on her own.

This wasn't a first, nor did she mind. Sure, she lived on Canyon Road but it wasn't like they ever really had any problems up here, except when there was a brush fire. If that happened, she knew what to grab and run, and that included Wacky, her seal point Siamese.

"Hey, Wacky," Marnie yelled. "Time to eat."

The sound of paws hitting the wooden stairs that led to the second floor had her laughing. She opened a package of Purina liver flavored Tender Vittles and wrinkled her nose.

"This smells nasty."

Wacky was probably the pickiest eater ever. He only liked this type of food, unless something dropped off the table. Once that happened, he attacked as if he was capturing live prey.

"Wacky! Food."

With a loud meow, Wacky wound around her legs, demanding his meal in an imperial manner. Marnie dumped the package into one of his bowls and while he was delicately eating, rinsed and refilled his water dish.

"Need to check the newspaper collection, Wacky," she said. "Keep an eye on things."

One thing Dad was known for was his packrat habit of keeping every newspaper that had a story about a local crime. Even if it was a small item on the back page, he had a copy in his home office. Marnie crept in there, hoping he didn't come home any time soon.

"Where are those copies from 1969?"

She started with the fourth pile on the floor but it was 1970. His filing system left a lot to be desired. Marnie finally located what she was looking for right next to the door. Only one copy of the *Monrovia News Post* was from 1969. It bore the headline *Family Murdered in Home on Littlejohn Road. Teenage Son Survives.*

"Found it." She plopped onto the floor and scanned the article. "Where is it?'

In seconds, she found what she wanted in the second paragraph.

Thomas and Marissa Jacobson were found in their bedroom, dead from shotgun wounds to their chests. Their younger children, eight-year-old Timothy and five-year-old Jennifer, died in a similar fashion. The Jacobson's fourteen-year-old son, Terry, survived without injury. He was in a basement bedroom and stumbled upon the devastation when he came upstairs for a drink of water, according to officers on the scene.

The murder had happened three blocks from where she lived. Garth was the Jacobson's next door neighbor while Tish and Les lived on Canyon Road, closer to Foothill Boulevard. The murders had been the talk of the town, with this article often misquoted. Marnie had tried to get her dad to tell her what he knew but he had told her that she was too young to be exposed to the goriness of what he'd seen.

"We were all in Terry's house a month before those murders," Marnie whispered. "It was for his birthday. None of us wanted to go but our parents said it wouldn't be right to ignore his invitation when he came to our parties."

What she had never mentioned was how much she had hated going to parties at Terry's house. That boy was creepy beyond belief and loved making smaller kids cry. Marnie had always had a sense that he had some kind of problem, but no one ever mentioned what it was.

She placed the paper carefully back where she'd found it. Marnie knew she could get a copy at the newspaper's office near the library. Her dad would never have to know that she'd come into his office when he wasn't home, but she didn't want anyone to know who she suspected of being responsible for Suzie's disappearance.

Sighing, she went into the kitchen, glancing at the clock. Still too early to go to bed. Her mom wouldn't be back from school until ten. Dad might show up close to midnight, if he didn't stay at the station all night.

"Not a big deal." She shivered, and it wasn't from the cold. "Really. Sort of. Yeah, it is a big deal. Something creepy is going on."

She could have called one of her friends but they were probably busy getting ready for graduation next week. She should organize her outfit for not only the ceremony but also the senior trip afterward. They were going to Disneyland this year, an all-night event she'd looked forward to since Christmas.

"Sure is quiet tonight." She moved aside the drapes and stared at the street. "Nobody is out. Weird."

Sure it was a school night, but it was unusual for no one to be walking on the sidewalk or driving past. She was so used to hearing movement outside that Marnie shivered from the lonely feeling. A glance at the cuckoo clock on the wall didn't bring any relief.

"Only seven-thirty," she muttered. "This is so weird. I've never been afraid to be in the house alone."

That was the only way she could think of to describe her nervousness. Marnie stepped back from the window and noticed a shadow moving around the bush near the front door.

"Who is that?"

Her heart thudding against her chest, she raced over to the front door and checked the locks.

"All good." She ran into the kitchen to check that door. "It's locked too."

Still, she was shaking from the thought that someone had been near the house. Maybe whoever it was had been watching her.

"I can always call Dad. He'll send someone by to check it out."

Hearing her own voice calmed her nerves somewhat. Marnie blew out a relieved breath and took a step. A warm, furry body rubbed against her leg.

"Argh!" she shrieked and looked down to see her cat sitting next to her with what could only be called a feline grin on his face. "Wacky, never do that again."

A muttered curse from beneath the window renewed her fear, only it was worse this time. Marnie clapped a hand over her mouth and raced out to the kitchen. She dialed the number to the police station and crouched down below the counter.

"Monrovia Police Department," an officer said. "How may I assist you?"

"I need to talk to my dad," Marnie said. "Detective Wildwood. Tell him it's really important."

"Just a minute please."

Tears rimming her eyes, she crouched closer to the floor and held the phone tightly to her ear. It seemed to take forever before she heard her dad's reassuring voice.

"What's up, kiddo?"

"Somebody was outside the living room window." She gulped in air. "Daddy, someone was outside our house. I thought I saw something but then Wacky scared me and I heard someone cursing."

"Are the doors locked?" His voice had gone to professional cop and he kept talking before she could answer. "Hang on, kiddo. I'm getting a car over there right now."

She could hear him hollering for the dispatcher to send every unit in the area to his house. Marnie released the tears. She realized that this wasn't how a potential detective was supposed to act, but she was really, really scared.

***

An hour later, the three police officers who had nearly beaten down the door before she let them in were leaving. Her dad had her in a warm hug and was rubbing her back. Marnie was still shaking from the scare she'd had.

"I'm so stupid," she said in a low voice. "Here I am, wanting to be a private investigator, and I get scared by some dummy creeping up on the house."

"It's a very normal reaction." Dad stepped back and stared into her eyes. "You did the right thing, Marnie. Always call the police if you think someone is outside the house. An officer would rather chase a phantom away than respond to a breaking and entering call."

She nodded. He'd told her this and many other things over the years. He was so cautious, but she needed more than his advice now... or maybe she did need his advice.

"Did anyone ever figure out how Suzie got from the south side of town to up here?" she asked.

"Nothing like a diversion to take your mind off a scare." He laughed. "No, we don't know how she got up here. Suzie might have walked; her parents said she didn't have many friends."

"That's the truth," Marnie said. "Could someone have been outside her house?"

"I never thought of that." He ruffled her hair, an action that normally annoyed her, but tonight it felt good. "Why don't you relax for a bit and then go to bed. I'll be in my study, making a few phone calls. I don't think whoever it was will come back."

She decided he was right. Marnie grabbed her copy of *Nancy Drew Secret of the Old Clock* and settled on the sofa. She glanced at the clock and noticed that it was a quarter to nine. She had about half an hour of reading before she had to go to bed.

Chapter Five

He panted from the effort of avoiding the police. His nerves were on edge and he was ready to make that spoiled brat pay. How dare she call the pigs on him? He wasn't doing anything wrong, just trying to figure out if she was going to be a problem.

You'll pay, Marnie Wildwood. I'll make sure that you pay before I'm done. Nobody does that to me. So what if I was looking in the window? I just wanted to find out what you know.

His presence on Canyon Road could be explained easily, but then any cop that stopped him would have his name and address. He couldn't let that happen. Nobody could know he prowled the area around Monrovia Canyon Park at night.

"Have to get home," he whispered, watching the three patrol cars leave the Wildwood house. "I'll take care of Marnie later."

Once the street was clear and the neighbors had gone back inside, he slipped out from where he'd been hiding. This house had been for sale for a couple of months. With no one living there, he was safe unless a cop decided to impress Detective

Wildwood and check out the only empty house on the street.

The Mastermind was just about to step onto the sidewalk when he heard footsteps approaching his location. He was still hidden by the tall hedge the owners had always refused to trim. He ducked down and used his hands to move aside some of the stubborn branches.

"You are not going to believe who I saw sneaking around last week."

The screechy voice belonged to Barbie Smith. Fear ran up and down his back, bringing on a cold sweat. He'd been careless last week when liberating some old coins from the Henderson's place a couple of blocks over. Not knowing the area had been his first mistake; continuing with the burglary when he heard people outside the house was the second. Yet, he'd thought at the time that he'd gotten away without anyone noticing him.

Even worse, he might have been noticed by the girl with the biggest mouth in the whole state. Everyone thought Barbie was a cute cheerleader with the well-known California girl looks—long, straight blonde hair, a perky nose, slender, and blue eyes. She got great grades in her classes but didn't tell anyone about them, a criminal act in his estimation. Her worst crime though was that she lived next door to the Henderson's.

"Who?" Nina Monroe asked.

Great, the two of them were hanging out together.

She sounded breathless. Of course, if she dropped about a hundred pounds, she might not have so much trouble walking. The dummy never did anything but hang out with people who hated her, and she was too stupid to figure that out. Her short-cut hair did nothing to complement her pudgy face. Fat rolls nearly obliterated her eyes.

He snickered. All his worry was for nothing. This dummy and the blonde bimbo couldn't have noticed him. They were too much into some guy singer, David Cassidy, to think about anything going on around them.

"Terry," Barbie said. "You know the baseball player."

He covered his mouth with a hand. She was so very, very wrong about almost everything. He had nothing to worry about.

"Do you mean the quarterback?" Nina asked.

"Oh yeah." Barbie giggled. "I keep forgetting he plays football. He's so scrawny and slow. I'm amazed the team did as well as it did this year with him on it."

"What did you see him doing?" Nina asked.

Red lights flashed and a car stopped on the street. He cowered behind the hedge, certain his days of sneaking around had been brought to an end.

"Girls," a police officer said. "We've had a problem with a prowler in the neighborhood. It might be a good idea if you went on home."

"Sure," they both called at the same time.

Barbie and Nina took off, walking away quickly. The officer drove slowly behind them.

"Damn." The Mastermind came up from his crouch. "I'll have to shut up those two. Can't have them running their lying mouths."

Once the street was clear, he took off, running back to the house he both loathed and couldn't stay away from. It drew him there, even after his family was gone. He hurried inside and headed up the stairs.

"Where have you been?" Uncle Jim asked.

"Out," The Mastermind said.

"I told you that you can't go running around. Did you pick up my medicine?"

"Pharmacy was closed." He walked up the stairs, comforted by the fact that his uncle couldn't follow him.

That accident hadn't happened like it should have. He'd rigged up the bottom two stairs in the basement to collapse when any weight was put on them, then complained about hearing something moving around down there. Uncle Jim had gone down to check and had fallen, but not hard enough to kill him. He'd only broken his right leg in half a dozen places and now had to rely on a cane to walk.

I'll do better the next time. No one will keep me from my money, especially that grumpy old man.

His mother's older brother was an even bigger jerk than she had been.

Chapter Six

Marnie met up with the rest of the Wildcat Crew at the friendship circle the next morning. All of them were pretty quiet while watching the rest of the students going through the motions of the last full week of school.

"What happened at your place last night?" Garth asked.

"I saw someone outside the house, hiding in the bushes," she said. "Guess I kind of panicked."

In the bright early June sunshine, she was really embarrassed by how she'd overreacted. Sure, it was kind of scary, but the doors had been locked and her dad had made sure it was nearly impossible to break into their house.

"What?" Les asked. "I heard the police going up Canyon last night but didn't think it was your place."

Barbie Smith and Nina Monroe walked past. They were talking excitedly.

"I can't believe you really saw him coming out of the Henderson's house," Nina said. "Did you tell the police?"

"Nah." Barbie shook her head. "It could have been him but it also could have been someone else. Who cares anyway? The Henderson's aren't coming back. I'm sure they didn't leave anything worth stealing in their house."

They walked away, still talking. Marnie stared at them, wondering if they knew something about the creeper.

"There's Brad," Garth said, pointing toward the snack shack. "Guess we need to get this over with."

Marnie frowned. She hadn't had time to talk to her dad about how they had to ask their questions. Not only that, but she was really sure Brad wasn't the person the police were looking for. She was certain another student in her class was the actual perpetrator. How to get everyone else to understand why she felt that way was going to be hard, which was why she was doing a job she found very disgusting.

"Hey." Brad stopped in front of them. "Heard about last night, Marnie. Really awful."

She ducked her head for a moment, pushing away the fear she'd felt last night. Her mind raced.

Was I wrong about Brad all along? He lives near Suzie. They're not friends, but he could still have seen her the night she disappeared.

No matter how much Marnie tried to justify her earlier thoughts that another person was responsible, she had to accept the fact that she could be wrong.

I hope I'm right. I really do.

"It was scary." She lifted her head, a solemn expression on her face. "Thankfully, Dad got the police there really fast."

She couldn't ask the question on the tip of her tongue, even if it would relieve some of her tension about how he knew what happened.

"How did you find out about last night?" Les asked, her eyes narrowing. "It's not like there was anything on the news this morning."

"Terry Jacobson told me right as I got off the bus," Brad said. "He was waiting on me."

He scratched his head and turned toward the student parking lot, where the last of the buses were heading into the barn.

"That's really strange," Garth said. "I didn't think Terry liked you."

"Yeah," Brad said in a low voice. "I thought it was strange too. Terry once told me that he wished I'd fall of the face of the earth."

Brad was the definition of a geek. Marnie couldn't help thinking that as she looked him up and down. While everyone else was wearing shorts and T-shirts or tank tops with sandals, he had on a pair of khaki pants, a checkered shirt (with the ever-present pocket protector loaded with pens, pencils, and a compass), and black loafers. His greasy light brown hair flopped over his glasses, which were in need of a serious cleaning. The only thing missing was the acne that had plagued him until last summer. Brad hadn't explained how that had disappeared, just smiled when anyone noticed that his face was finally blemish free.

"Sit down." Marnie patted the stone bench beside her, scraping her elbow against the retaining wall behind her. "We need to talk."

Panic flashed across Brad's face. He glanced at each of them in turn, taking in their serious expressions.

"What's up?" he asked.

"We need to talk," she said. "It's really nothing, Brad. Just a couple of things we need to clear up."

"Is this coming from Wildcat Crew or the police?" Brad sat between Marnie and Les. "Are you guys trying to set me up?"

This was the hardest thing Marnie had ever done. Sure, she knew when she decided on what career she wanted, she would have to do uncomfortable things.

Now that she was faced with that reality, she was scared that she would mess up and make the situation worse.

"Wildcat Crew is asking," Tish said. "Yeah, we're going to tell the police what you tell us. We're doing this as a favor for them, but we don't think you had anything to do with Suzie's disappearance."

Brad leaned backward, resting against the retaining wall around the flagpole that had a bed of petunias surrounding it. His fingers moved on their own accord, fiddling with the edges of an already battered five subject notebook.

"You should suspect me," he said in a low voice. "I live only a couple of houses away from her."

That statement startled Marnie. She had never expected Brad to admit that and was at a loss on how to approach him about what he knew.

"Okay," Garth said. "Tell us about Suzie."

"Like what?" Brad asked.

"Her parents said that she argued with them," Les said. "Did you know about that?"

Brad sighed. He pushed his glasses up on his nose.

"Yeah. The whole neighborhood knew about that," he said. "Those arguments got real loud all the time. Sometimes... sometimes..." Brad gulped. "Sometimes, they would scream at her that she was an ungrateful brat, for wanting stuff she didn't need."

"Like what?" Tish asked.

The bell rang for their first class of the day. None of them moved. For the rest of their time at Monrovia High, they were excused from this class.

"Suzie wanted to wear the same clothes as everyone else," Brad said. "She didn't like being different. That's why she wants to attend the Fashion Institute in New York."

"She wants to be a designer?" Marnie asked.

"A model," Brad said. "That's what was really weird. Suzie doesn't look like a model, but that's her dream."

Marnie shook her head. She'd been down to Suzie's house for a party that was so old-fashioned nobody had much fun. At fourteen, they were way beyond a piñata and musical chairs, with boys on one side of the room and girls on the other side. But Mr. and Mrs. Calderone had insisted on putting on an event that was more appropriate for third graders.

"What is it about her parents?" Garth asked. "How come they act like they do?"

"I don't know if I can tell you," Brad said. "Suzie made me promise to keep that a secret."

"Brad." Marnie touched his shoulder. "We need to know everything you know. Suzie has been gone for two days. Nobody has seen her since she left her house."

He sighed again and shook his head. Brad stared up at the sky, worry etched into his face.

"Do you have to tell your dad about this?" he asked.

"It depends on what you tell me," she said. "If it's important and can help him find her, I will have to tell him."

"I just don't know if it's worth breaking a promise to tell you," he said.

"We'd have to do that," Tish said. "Especially if that information helps the police find her."

Brad lowered his head and stared at his hands. His fingers twitched constantly. Marnie was worried they were about to hear something really awful, but she couldn't figure out what it could be.

"I hate breaking promises. Feels like I lied to the person," he said in a low voice. "But…" He looked at all of them again. "Are you sure you have to know?"

Marnie wasn't sure exactly what Brad was about to reveal, and she was certain he would be doing that very soon, but she had a feeling it was very important.

"Yes," she said firmly. "We have to know, Brad. What if this secret is the reason Suzie disappeared? What if she's in real trouble?"

"That's what I'm afraid of," he said. "Okay. Here goes. But you have to promise that you'll only tell your dad, Marnie. No one else, especially the people around here, at school. They can't know this."

"Okay." Marnie glanced at the others.

"Sure," Tish said.

"Not their business," Les said.

"I'm not saying a word," Garth said.

Marnie breathed a sigh of relief. She had been afraid that her friends wouldn't go along with Ben, and she was certain he had really important information.

"It's like this." Ben leaned his arms against his knees and stared at the ground. "Suzie's not an only child. Her parents lied about that when they moved here in the middle of eighth grade. And they aren't from Poughkeepsie, New York."

"Really?" Marnie stared at him in astonishment. "Do you know where they came from?"

"Beverly Hills," he said. "They moved here after her older brother and sister ran away. The Calderones aren't what they appear to be. Her dad isn't an insurance salesman. Her mom has never spent much time at home, until George and Christine took off."

This information was explosive. The Calderones made a huge thing about how honest they were. Most of Suzie's trouble came from how they made her dress and behave like a little girl from the fifties. She'd endured so much teasing about that since the disastrous party.

I have to call Dad as soon Ben finishes telling us the whole story.

"Why did Christine and George leave," Tish asked. "Were they in trouble?"

"Not yet," Brad said. "They were into marijuana, liked smoking it."

Marnie hissed in a breath. This was really bad. She wasn't sure what she wanted to hear next. Her dad had told her that people into drugs were a danger to society, and marijuana was a drug.

"George was selling pot to the kids at school," Brad said. "It was a private school in Beverly Hills. He was caught by the police and Christine tried to take the pot and run."

"Oh no." Les shook her head. "But that's not so bad that their parents have to come down on Suzie and treat her like she's going to do the same thing."

"You know." Ben looked up. "You're right. And that's exactly what happened. Suzie sometimes comes off as a jerk. She talks about what she sees and hears, because she's trying to get people to like her, but she shouldn't be treated like a baby because her brother and sister messed up."

"I agree," Marnie said. "Do you think Suzie might have gone to her brother and sister?"

"Her sister might know where she is," Ben said. "But... well, her brother's in prison. He wasn't just into pot. George was dealing heroin too."

The information Brad was giving them put a lot of things into perspective. Marnie needed to know only one more thing.

"Where does Christine live now?" she asked.

"Right here in Monrovia," Brad said. "She lives in those pink apartments on Foothill."

"Is her last name Calderone?" Garth asked.

The others stared at him in shock. He shrugged his shoulders.

"What? People have changed their names if they want to hide their past," he said. "Maybe Suzie's parents did that."

"They did." Brad nodded. "Christine's last name is Adams."

Marnie jumped to her feet. "I have to tell Dad this, Brad. He needs to know, so they can talk to Suzie's sister."

"Kind of figured that," Brad said. "It's okay. I realize now that it was wrong to hold all that back."

"One more thing," Garth said. "Did you see Suzie the night she disappeared?"

"She was running north, toward Mayflower," Brad said. "I saw someone come out of the bushes near her living room windows right after she took off, but I couldn't see his face."

"A man?" Tish asked.

"Yeah, or a really tall, skinny woman," Brad said. "But I'm pretty sure it was a man."

"Why?" Marnie asked.

"Uh…" His face turned bright red. "I just know he was."

She had to smother a giggle. Marnie was pretty sure she had figured out why Brad was sure it was a man. Now, all she had to do was find her dad.

Chapter Seven

Marnie rushed into the main office and waited for the woman behind the desk to finish a phone call.

"May I make a call, please, Mrs. Watkins?" she asked. "It's really important. Something my dad asked me to do."

"Do you need some privacy?" Mrs. Watkins asked.

"That would probably be a good idea." Marnie nodded.

"It'll be a couple of minutes." Mrs. Watkins nodded at the chairs on a wall beside the door. "Take a seat, please."

Sitting still was probably the hardest thing Marnie had done so far today. Her nerves were still on edge from last night and she was bursting from what she'd learned about the Calderones. Imagine a family changing their names because their older children got into drugs. And that one part Brad still had to explain really bothered her. She could hear his voice resonating in her head now.

"Her dad isn't an insurance salesman. Her mom has never spent much time at home, until George and Christine took off."

What kind of family changed not only their name and abandoned two of their children, but also lied about what their occupations were? Just who were the Calderones? Or were they the Adams?

I don't understand this at all. Why didn't Suzie's parents tell Dad all this? He would have never asked us to talk to Brad until he'd checked out George and Christine. There hasn't been enough time for him to have done that.

It seemed to take forever for one of the counselors to leave their office. Marnie was bouncing her foot up and down. She was worried that she would miss her next class, Greek Mythology. She loved that class and the teacher as well.

"Marnie?" Mrs. Watkins pointed at the far office. "You can use the phone now."

"Thanks." She dashed into the room and quickly dialed the station.

"Monrovia Police Department," the desk sergeant said. "How may I assist you?"

"Hi, this is Marnie Wildwood," she said. "I need to talk to Dad. He knows what it's about."

"Hang on, Marnie."

She heard the click of the phone being put on hold. Her nerves were drawn so tightly that she couldn't sit still, but this phone didn't have a long extension cord on it, so she was forced to hunch over the desk and keep a wary eye out for anyone who might eavesdrop on her conversation.

"Hey, kiddo." Dad sounded tired; he hadn't been home when she woke up this morning. "Do you have something for me?"

"Yes!" She nearly shouted the words and then cast a worried look at the outer office, lowering her voice. "It's huge, Dad."

"Hey, quiet down in here," he said. "I'm on the phone."

She giggled.

"Okay," Dad said. "What did you find out?"

"Did you know the Calderones changed their names when they moved here from Beverly Hills" she asked.

"Excuse me?"

"They changed their names," Marnie said. "Suzie has an older brother and sister, George and Christine. They left home after George was caught with pot at their high school and Christine tried to take it away from the police."

She could hear him scribbling notes. Marnie waited for her dad to respond.

"Do you know their last name before they changed it?" he asked. "I can get the information, but it might take a long time and a court order."

"Uh, yeah. It's Adams," she said. "But that's not the most important information we got from Brad. There's a lot more."

"Hang on," he said. "I need another notebook."

She could hear him snapping his fingers and imagined someone tossing him a notebook. Marnie heard the bell announcing the beginning of second period. She groaned quietly. Missing this class could get her into trouble.

"I heard that bell," Dad said. "I know you want to get to class, but this is pretty important. You have information the Calderones didn't give us. We might be able to locate Suzie much faster if we can figure out where her brother and sister live."

"I understand," she said, letting her unhappiness at having to miss part of her class out in her voice. "Her sister, Christine, lives in those pink apartments up on Foothill."

"Good, good," he muttered. "I'll go over and talk to her as soon as we hang up. What about her brother."

"Brad said that George was in prison," Marnie said. "For dealing heroin, I think is what he told us."

"I can find him easily then." Dad blew out his breath. "Thanks, kiddo. This is exactly what I needed."

She almost held back the last bit of information. It could wait until he got home tonight.

Can it wait? What if the creeper at Suzie's house is the same guy that was at my house? Dad really needs to know this.

"Brad saw Suzie leave," she said. "She was running toward Mayflower."

"That's a start on how she got to the north end of town," he said.

"There's more." She bit hard on her lip, wondering how she could convey to her dad exactly how Brad knew the creeper was a man.

"What?"

"He saw a man leaving from the bushes in front of the Calderone's living room windows," she said. "And he's really sure it's a man."

"Why?"

"Well... because... Dad, he blushed and just said he knew it was a man," she said. "Figure it out!"

"Oh." He snorted with laughter. "I get it. Go on to the attendance office. I'll call ahead and get you a pass to class. Thanks."

She hung up the phone and grabbed her notebooks and purse. Marnie hurried toward the attendance office, housed in a wooden building behind the one she was in. She hoped she didn't run into the principal or the cop on campus on her way. It would be pretty hard to explain why she was out of class.

Chapter Eight

At the end of the day, Wildcat Crew met again in the friendship circle. Brad was with them. While the others kicked back and relaxed, Marnie paced in front of them.

"What did the note you got from your dad say?" Brad asked.

"That he'd meet us here as soon as school let out." She peered at the parking lot and groaned. "How can anyone get in through that mess?"

As was usual this time of year, every student who drove was trying to get out at the same time. The long line of cars inching toward the exit didn't seem to be moving. Anyone trying to enter would have to wait on those who'd pulled out into the line and were blocking the lane leading to the reserved spots moved.

"Carefully," Tish said with a giggle. "Are we really that bad when we leave?"

"Usually," Garth said. "Sometimes, we're worse."

Marnie had to admit that none of them liked hanging around school after the last bell rang. There was so much to do, not just homework, but hanging out at the burger place or Shakey's Pizza Parlor a few blocks away. Sometimes, they would head up into the mountains and hike during the spring and summer months, until it was time to go home for dinner. Their best after school activity, no matter what time of year it was, was to haunt the library, hoping they had new books that might interest them. None of them thought twice about creeping into the long line to get out of the parking lot and onto Madison Avenue. It was worse if someone had to turn left, since no one gave an inch if they were already on the street.

"Okay, you're right," she admitted. "We really are worse sometimes."

They were all laughing in a matter of seconds. Marnie wondered how they could do that with Suzie still missing and all the information they'd discovered about her family. Knowing her parents had not only abandoned their other children but also changed their names made her wonder exactly why they'd taken such extreme measures. Even her dad had been surprised by that information and he'd told her and her mom that nothing much could surprise him after the Manson Family rampage.

"Losers."

The disgusted tone and unprovoked attack had all of them instantly sobering. Marnie glared at Terry Jacobson. She'd never liked him; had hated going to his house when his family was alive for parties. Since that awful night, he'd become even weirder than he was before, making comments that had a lot of people angry at him.

"What is your problem?" Les asked.

"That I have to put up with all of you," he said, flipping a hand at Brad. "That jerk should be in jail, but he's sitting here acting like he didn't attack Suzie Calderone. I wonder what her parents would think if they hear about this." He glared at Marnie. "With a pig's daughter too."

She jerked back in surprise. Very few students at MHS used the word "pig" to describe the police. Most thought it was really rude. Others didn't want to hear someone yelling at them for putting down the police.

He's so angry. She examined Terry's build, listened to his voice, and didn't like what she was seeing or hearing. *Terry looks a lot like that creeper that was at my house. He sounds like he's trying to start trouble.*

She was so caught up in trying to figure him out that she didn't notice someone approaching them until she heard a familiar voice.

"Hey, kids," Dad said. "What's going on?"

Terry ran off without saying anything. Garth took a step toward the football player, but Les stopped him by grabbing his arm.

"Don't," she said. "That's what Terry wants, you or one of us to go after him. He'll have a reason to beat on someone."

"Okay." Dad moved into the center of the group. "What's going on?"

"Nothing," Marnie said. "Just Terry being his usual jerky self."

"He's always like that?" he asked.

"Unless he knows an adult is around," Tish said. "Then he's all Mr. Nice Guy, wouldn't ever do anything wrong because someone murdered my family and the police can't figure out who."

"Interesting," Dad said. "So, what am I keeping you from today?"

"Brainstorming session at Shakey's," Garth said. "We were going to split a pizza and talk about everything we've learned. Brad too."

"Good." Dad nodded. "The traffic jam seems to have cleared up. You kids go on ahead and order the pizza. I'll meet you up there after I chat with your principal. Mr. Jameson needs to know a few things about Suzie and her family."

"That doesn't sound good," Marnie said.

"I'll explain later." He kissed her forehead. "Thanks for letting me have all that information. We've contacted Christine and she was very helpful. I'll explain it all in a bit."

He strode toward the main building. Watching him go, Marnie and her friends headed for the parking lot.

***

An hour later, they were all chomping down on a pepperoni pizza and sipping Cokes from frosty glasses. Dad finally came through the door. He pointed at the girl behind the cash register.

"Bring another pizza on over here and another pitcher of Coke," he said. "I'll pay when you do."

"Yes, sir," the girl said. "Have you heard anything about Suzie yet?"

Marnie would never describe her dad as a memorable person. She thought of him as someone who looked so ordinary that he was forgettable, not at all like a square-jawed police detective portrayed in the movies. Yet, no matter where he went, Dad was recognized by half the town. She wasn't sure how to explain that.

"Nothing yet," Dad said. "We won't give up looking for her until she's home safe."

He slid onto the bench and sat beside Brad.

"Okay, son." Dad touched Brad's hand. "You're off the hook. I talked to your parents and they've verified what Marnie told me. You were in your house all night when Suzie disappeared."

"Thank you," Brad said. "Did what I told Wildcat Crew about her family help?"

"More than you realize." Dad waited while the cashier set their second pizza and pitcher of Coke on the table, along with a clean glass. "Thanks," he said and handed her a twenty. "Keep the change."

"Thank you!" The cashier practically skipped back to the register.

"Ah, food." He put a slice on a plate and poured some of the drink into his cup. "First, we'll talk about Christine. She had a very interesting story."

He took a huge bite of the pizza and chewed as if he hadn't eaten since breakfast. Marnie was losing patience. She needed to know what he'd discovered.

"Well." She sipped more of her drink.

"Well, very deep subject," Dad said after swallowing. "Holds water."

"Daaaaaaad!"

"Okay, no more bad jokes."

The others were snorting with laughter.

"Here's what Christine told me," he said. "George wasn't arrested for being involved with heroin. He wasn't the owner of that marijuana he was caught with at school either."

"What?" Brad asked. "Suzie told me that. How could she be wrong?"

"Probably because she was told that story by her parents," Dad said. "Michael and Lisa Adams are wanted on charges of heroin trafficking and growing marijuana on the hill behind their old home in Beverly Hills. They may have claimed to have changed their names to Calderone, but there is no official record of that."

Marnie was stunned. She'd never been this close to a serious criminal in her life. Despite that issue, she still wanted to be an investigator.

"What are you saying?" Tish asked.

"The Calderones, the Adams actually, are criminals," Dad said. "They rebuilt their lives, creating a fake and nearly untraceable background in order to avoid prosecution. Unfortunately, when we attempted to confront them with their lies, they had disappeared."

"What are you saying?" Garth asked. "They took off when their youngest daughter is missing?"

"That's exactly what I'm saying," Dad said. "So, you kids are all eighteen now. Which means you're adults. This is an official request from the Monrovia Police Department. Would you like to assist us with this case?"

"Will you tell us about Christine and George?" Tish asked. "I think they're important."

"You'll have all the information I have," Dad said, standing. "I'll be right back. Talk and make a decision while I'm gone."

He took off toward the bathrooms. Marnie turned to her friends, and she now included Brad as part of their team. Since talking to him earlier, she'd come to realize that he wasn't the person she'd thought he was.

Chapter Nine

"What do you think?" Les asked. "Is your dad serious?"

Marnie nodded. She'd thought about that a lot since he walked away from the table. At first, she thought he was going to use the bathroom, but she could see him on the pay phone between the restrooms. Marnie figured he was getting information from the station. At times, she wondered how weird it was with all the really neat stuff that had come out lately—LCD watches, pocket calculators, and eight track players for music—all these had made their lives so much better, in her opinion. But no one had come up with a way to make a phone call without having one attached physically to the wires.

Maybe that will happen someday.

Although she and her friends liked to think they had a lot of great new things and the world was changing for the better, they'd faced the grim reality that wasn't really true.

There's been a lot of bad stuff happening for a while.

Or course, images of the police investigation into the murders in Beverly Hills in 1969 and the Manson Family were always at the top of her personal list of super bad stuff. There were also events like the Kent State shooting in 1970 and the ongoing Watergate investigation that was dominating the news. Both let her know that her safe and secure world wasn't that way anymore. Marnie wasn't sure what the future held but she hoped it would be much better than what they had now in some ways.

One thing she could count on was that the people like her dad, police officers all over the world, were doing their best to protect honest citizens. She knew for a fact that he never made an offer like he had without being sincere about it.

"Yeah." Marnie nodded. "He's very serious."

The idea that they were being accepted as investigators before they even started taking college classes scared her a lot. There were so many things that could go wrong.

"I say we do it," Tish said. "We don't want the police thinking we're scared. Do we?"

Everyone stared at her with their mouths open. Marnie snapped hers shut and thought about it. Yes, it was a scary situation, especially with a creeper around. But they couldn't afford to say it was too hard and they were scared.

I am scared. This is too weird. Nothing, except for Terry's family being murdered, has happened like this in Monrovia that I can remember.

Still, this was what she wanted to do with her life. No other occupation appealed to her. It was more than her dad being a cop, just like it was a lot more than Tish having a criminal defense attorney for a dad, while Garth's was a prosecutor. Les always said her family was the odd one out. Her parents ran a pharmacy on Myrtle Avenue.

We can do this. Marnie nodded. *It's what we've wanted since our freshman year.*

"You're right, Tish," she said. "We can't tell the police no. We'll never get a second chance with them."

"Well, I sure don't want to be the one they call the next time the football team puts the trashcans on the library's roof," Garth said. "I don't think we'll ever live that down."

"You're right." Brad looked at everyone. "Maybe I'm not planning on being a police officer, or an investigator, but helping out now seems important. Suzie isn't the person most of you see at school. She has dreams and wants to be normal."

Marnie glanced at him. A red flush covered his cheeks. Her eyes widened.

He's in love with Suzie. Bet she hasn't noticed either. She rolled her eyes. *How can she notice anything except her horrible family life?*

"We'll do it," Les said. "Guess we figured it out just in time. Your dad's coming back, Marnie."

They all grabbed another piece of pizza and chomped into them. Marnie was giggling around her slice when her dad sat back down and stared at the empty platter.

"At least I got a couple of slices," he said. "So, what did you decide?"

"We'll do it," Garth said. "What is it you need us to handle?"

"You need to talk to Suzie's sister," Dad said. "Listen to what she has to say about her family. I know all of you are old enough to do this without your parents' permission, but I need to speak to them first. This isn't a pretty or easily solved situation."

"Okay," Marnie said. "But one thing first." She leaned forward, propping her chin in her hands. "What happened to George Adams? All you said is that he wasn't arrested and didn't go to prison."

"Yes, I did say that," Dad said. "We don't know what happened to George. Christine doesn't know. That's why she walked away from her parents' house in Beverly Hills. They took George with them one day. The parents came back. He didn't, and they wouldn't say what had happened, just that if Christine and Suzie didn't toe the line and keep their mouths closed, they would join their brother."

Marnie straightened and glanced at the others. They all had shocked expressions. She figured her face looked just like theirs.

This is weirder than anything we've ever experienced.

"Changed your minds?" Dad asked. "It's not bad if you don't want to get involved."

She knew if she spoke first and told him that they would help, the others would go along with her. Marnie hated that she was often considered the leader of their group; she preferred to think of them as equal.

"No way," Les said. "I'm still in."

"Me too," Tish said. "This is intriguing."

"I want to know what happened to Suzie," Brad said. "I'm in."

"Same here," Garth said.

Everyone looked at Marnie. She considered all the strange events that had happened in the last couple of days before nodding.

"Yeah, I'm in," she said.

Chapter Ten

He was sitting near the video games at Shakey's, listening to the conversation. Those fools had no idea who he was. None of them had considered that anyone would pay attention to what they were saying. All they were thinking about was Suzie's loser family. He'd long ago figured out that they were dealers. What other way could that fat broad get such good pot?

Dumb broad. She didn't even figure out that I stole her stash while she was unconsciousness. All she's done since coming around is whimper for food and water. I hate her.

Unfortunately, for him to achieve the glory he desired, he would have to step up his plan. There were only eight days left to find and capture four men and two more women. The numbers had to be perfect. He couldn't deviate from what the Manson Family had done—only he would use a different method of getting rid of his prey. They would think they had a chance to live, until he delivered the death blow.

"Well, it's time to go," the pig said. "Can't stay here all night eating pizza."

"Mom's going to be so mad," Marnie said. "We should have saved some for her, Dad."

"She's taking her last final tonight," he said. "Won't be home until about ten. I think she and her friends over there will stop for something on the way."

"Marnie, we don't have school tomorrow," Les said. "Stay at my house tonight. We can brainstorm."

"Can't," Marnie said. "Have to take care of Wacky. He doesn't like Dad."

"That's the truth." He kissed the top of her head. "Don't be too long. I'm going home."

Once everyone had gone, The Mastermind remained in his corner for a while longer. He still had some pizza and didn't want anyone remembering him as the person who ordered something and left before finishing it.

Marnie will be home with her dad tonight. I can deliver a message she'll never forget, but I have to wait for her mom to get home. He smiled and folded a slice in half, stuffing it into his mouth. *I can wait. I'm very patient.*

He waited until he could see that they'd all left. That loser, Brad, took off with Garth, which bothered The Mastermind. He wasn't sure what those two were plotting and going near Garth's place was dangerous. His dad had private security around the house all the time, after having several threats made against his family.

That's what he gets for dumping people in jail for stupid stuff.

He left Shakey's and headed back toward Canyon Road, remembering at the last second that his beat-up Rambler that had belonged to his parents would stick out on a street where most people's vehicles were at the most five years old.

"Damn my uncle," he whispered as he pulled into the driveway of the house where'd he'd done his best work. "I want that money. He will give it to me this weekend."

***

Several hours later, he crept from the house and cut through yards where the homeowners didn't have pets. The whole area was very quiet, too quiet for a Friday night. Curtains were drawn tightly against windows, allowing very little light to leach out.

What is going on? Why are people closing their curtains? Has someone discovered who I am?

His anger rose yet again at how he was being thwarted. Everyone was against him. He had no chance to complete his mission unless he turned Monrovia into a war zone—where he was the one in control.

First, I make those Wildwoods scared out of their minds. That pig won't be concentrating on finding Suzie if his own family is being targeted.

A smile on his face, he returned to his home and gathered supplies, at the last minute preparing a very smelly special surprise for that smarty-pants, Marnie. His footsteps echoed off the empty streets as he hurried to his target. To his amazement, no one peeked out the curtains to see who was out and about at this hour. He stopped in front of Marnie's house and noticed that everything was dark.

Good. They'll never hear a thing.

Determination in his step, he walked around to the driveway and spotted the red Camaro, which was what he'd wanted. A girl didn't need a muscle car like this. She was a spoiled brat.

Time to make her pay.

He was panting and sweaty an hour later as he stepped back to admire his artistry. No one would ever drive this vehicle again. Marnie would be forced into walking or waiting on someone to give her a ride. He might volunteer for the job, even though he hated her guts.

Maybe I can take her to my special place once I convince her to get into my car. She'll soon figure out she's not so special.

The sound of two girls talking nearby sent him sprinting quietly to the edge of the house. He peered out at the sidewalk.

"We have to tell someone," Nina Monroe said. "This is wrong."

"We can't," Barbie smith said. "Who would believe us? Everyone thinks he's such a great kid for surviving that awful thing four years ago."

They were talking about him. Of that, he was certain. Dropping the rest of his supplies quietly into a trashcan, he snuck out and walked quietly behind the girls, shadowing them alongside the houses and hedgerows. They were headed in the direction of the canyon. All he needed them to do was get beyond the houses and he could capture them.

After fifteen minutes of walking, the girls stopped at the path leading to his hiding place. He was grinning. They would soon understand that he was powerful and they were his pawns.

"Are you sure no one will figure out where we are?" Nina asked. "That weed you got is great, but I don't want to get caught. I'll lose my scholarship."

"Don't worry." Barbie stepped onto the path. "Nobody remembers this place is up here."

Nobody but your worst nightmare, Cheerleader Barbie!

Once they were inside the abandoned house, he waited a couple of minutes. They were so into getting high that they didn't hear him until it was too late. He punched out Barbie first. Nina managed to scream for a couple of panic stricken seconds before he silenced her. Carrying their limp bodies to where his other captive awaited her punishment took almost half an hour.

"Please." Suzie was weeping. "Let me… us go. We didn't do anything to you."

He walked away with saying a word.

Chapter Eleven

Marnie was startled out of a deep sleep. She rubbed the sleep from her eyes and glanced at her partially open window. Dad had wanted her to shut it tightly, in case the creeper came back, but she needed it open. The fresh air wafting through her room always helped her sleep.

"What was that?"

Hearing her voice in the too quiet house startled her. Movement from the bottom of the bed and an irritated meow brought a smile to her face.

"Sorry, Wacky." She stroked his back. "Must have been a nightmare."

She lay back down but was jerked fully awake when the sound of a terrorized scream came through her open window. Marnie jumped out of the bed, grabbed her robe and put it on, and raced down to her parents' bedroom.

"Dad?" She knocked on the door. "I can hear screaming from the canyon."

"I heard it." His weary voice came from behind the door. "Your mom is awake too. Go on down to the kitchen. We'll meet you there."

She ran downstairs and turned on the kitchen light. A glance at the clock made her really happy she didn't have school today. It was two-thirty. The fear still rushing through her from that scream guaranteed she'd be awake for a couple of hours at least.

"Coffee." Marnie measured out the water and coffee beans, putting everything into the electric drip pot on the kitchen counter, and turned it on. "Great. That'll be ready soon."

Although not a coffee drinker, she needed a cup this morning to release the tension running through her. This case was far weirder than she ever thought any investigation could be. Once the Manson Family was sent to prison, everyone she knew was relieved and happy that they wouldn't have to endure anything so frightening again. Yet, a mere four—*It hasn't even been a full four years yet*—three years and ten months later, they were experiencing the same kind of dread that had their parents keeping them close and feeling smothered back then.

Marnie leaned against the sink and stared out the kitchen window. Although she couldn't see much beyond the puddle of light spilling through the glass, she was bothered by an image she couldn't quite understand.

"Is that coffee I smell?" Mom asked.

"Yeah." Marnie turned away from the counter and wondered what was bugging her. "Where's Dad?"

"He stopped in his study to call the station and have them send a couple of units up here." Mom stood beside Marnie. "What's that in the driveway?"

Marnie spun around and peered through the window again. Her eyes widened in horrified shock. "My car!" she cried. "What happened to my car?"

Spinning around, she took a step toward the door. Dad came into the kitchen.

"What about your car?" he asked.

"It looks like someone trashed it," she said.

He ran out the door. Marnie followed him.

"Stay inside," Mom called. "Whoever did that might still be out there."

"I'm with Dad," Marnie yelled back.

Once she stood in front of her 1968 red Camaro, her heart sank to her toes. The damage was so bad she didn't think it could be fixed.

"What in the world?" Dad walked slowly around her car. "Did you lock your car when you got home?"

She had to think about that. Marnie didn't usually lock her car. There was no real reason to, unless she went to Los Angeles with her friends. Monrovia was safe. Nothing really happened here, and if it did, the police were quick to find the person responsible and put them in jail.

"I don't think so," she said. "Why?"

"Just asking." Dad ran a hand through his thick, short hair. "Honey, this is going to be a total loss. I just don't see any way to repair the damage."

A tear ran out of her eye. Her parents had always been good about letting her use their vehicles, until she received this as an early graduation gift a few weeks ago. The independence and freedom she'd felt from the first moment, along with the pride that they had understood how much she loved this particular model, had yet to fade. Despite having owned the Camaro for such a short time, she washed and waxed the exterior and vacuumed out the interior every on Saturday morning. Smudges were wiped away and every inch of the chrome was polished until it shone.

"Who did this?" There was a hitch in her voice.

Shaving cream and eggs were splattered all over the exterior. The windows were open but she remembered closing them.

I should have locked the doors, even if I did park in our driveway.

The radio antenna was nowhere in sight. Aware that she didn't have shoes on, she walked in a wide circle, examining what had been done. The gas tank door was open, with a clear plastic tube hanging from it. Dad used his handkerchief to remove that and sniffed.

"Bleach," he said. "Oh, honey, this is really terrible. Even if we could afford to pay for the damage to the body, I don't think we can fix bleach in the gas tank."

More tears dripped from her eyes. They got worse once Mom joined them, clad in a sweatsuit and carrying a flashlight. Dad shined the flashlight through the windows and Marnie nearly threw up.

The interior looked as if a spoiled child had thrown eggs, baked beans, and what appeared to be cookie sprinkles everywhere. A rotten stench wafted out into the early morning air.

"Is that—" Mom covered her nose with an arm. "Good grief, that smells like poop."

"It is," Dad said, turning around and holding out an arm.

A glance at the rear seat solved the mystery of where the radio antenna was; sticking out of a pile of poop.

This is more than the actions of a spoiled child. Marnie gulped back the new tears threatening to roll out of her eyes. *This was done to hurt me.*

Dad held out an arm she knew would be comforting. Marnie shook her head and backed away. She didn't want consolation. She didn't want anyone to see her crying over losing a car, but that would probably have to happen, once Dad had an officer come to take a report. All she really wanted right now was to crawl back into her bed and snuggle with Wacky, until the grief about losing a gift that meant so much abated.

Lights swung into their driveway, both the standard vehicle type and flashing red ones. The three of them turned to see a patrol car parking behind the Camaro.

"Detective." Officer James Hamilton stepped out onto the driveway. "We couldn't find any trace of someone in trouble up here." He approached them. "Can you be more specific—" The officer stared at Marnie's car in horror. "What in the world?"

"Get some people out here to take evidence," Dad said. "It appears this is becoming very personal. Tell them to be prepared for some very nasty stuff in the interior."

"Yes, sir." Officer Hamilton gulped. "Sir, perhaps the chief is right. This looks very personal to me too. I know I wouldn't want my teenage daughter to experience something like this. Maybe you should let a patrol car be stationed in your driveway until we figure out what's going on."

"You might be right," Dad said, glancing at Marnie and her mom. "My family's safety has to come first."

"What about the scream?" Marnie asked.

"We didn't find anything," Officer Hamilton repeated. "It might have been a coyote in the hills."

"It wasn't," she said. "I'm sure it was a person and they were in the hills. I'm pretty sure it came from there."

She turned and pointed at an area of the canyon where there wasn't anything except brush and rocks. The only place she could think of this close to her house where she could hear a scream was a rutted track that led off the road and disappeared after going up and around a curve. None of them had ever gone down to investigate that area, mostly because there seemed to be nothing to see.

"There's nothing up there," Hamilton said. "Nobody would be hiking after dark. Would they?"

Before anyone could respond, his radio crackled.

"All units in the vicinity of Canyon Road," the dispatcher said. "We have a report of two missing teenagers. Barbie Smith and Nina Monroe haven't been seen by their families since approximately eight o'clock last night."

"Oh, Lord." Mom grabbed Marnie's arm. "Get inside the house right this very minute." She faced Dad. "What is going on, Jonathon?"

He strode toward the vehicle. "I'm about to find out, Marty."

Marnie ran after him. She wasn't about to quit on this case now. Deep in her heart, she was beginning to think the mysterious creeper, whoever trashed her car, and the person responsible for the three disappearances was the same individual.

Her only problem now? How to prove that.

Chapter Twelve

The sun rose slowly over the San Gabriel Mountains. Marnie wore jeans, a tank top, and hiking boots with thick socks. She was standing at the railing, sipping her fifth cup of coffee since discovering her destroyed car, and staring at the vegetation covering the hills above her house.

"Are you eating breakfast this morning?" Mom joined her. "I made blueberry muffins, since there are so many people here."

She was wearing an outfit similar to Marnie's. Movement from the driveway took her attention away from the hills and Marnie faced the bustling activity going on. Men scurried around her car, being careful not to step on potential evidence. A group of about half a dozen officers stood in a circle around Dad, throwing questions at him and nodding at his replies. Nearby, the chief was talking to some of the other detectives, who had shown up after Dad called them.

"This is getting very serious," the chief said. "We have one of our detectives being threatened." He pointed at her car. "And that was a threat. I don't care what the individual who did this says once we apprehend him—a threat has been made."

"Or her," one of the men said. "Might have been a woman."

"Or her." The chief nodded. "We also have three missing teenage girls in this area. I have no idea what this is all about and I don't want to hear any excuses. We are going to scour this canyon from one end to the other. That will be up to the uniformed officers. I've already contacted LAPD about having their search and rescue dogs brought in, but that won't happen for a few hours. You, gentlemen, will be going from door to door. You will speak to everyone in each home, on every street, and see if anyone else heard this scream. If they did, you need to have them point out to you where they thought it was coming from."

"Sir." Dad joined the chief. "The canyon not only amplifies sound, it can bounce it around. Even if these people are certain they know where the scream was coming from, they might be wrong."

Marnie took another sip of her cooling coffee. She was taking in every detail of the investigation, in order to learn how to better hone her own skills. Some of it looked incredibly boring, but she understood the reasoning behind the time being spent discussing what had happened, who had to go where, and how long they would conduct the search before calling it off.

"Marnie, I really don't want you going up in those hills alone," Mom said. "It's not just because of the inherent danger involved in a search like this, but you may have been targeted by this… this… person."

"Do you mean the jerk that trashed my car?" Marnie asked. "Or the freak who peeked in the living room windows? Or the person who made Suzie, Barbie, and Nina disappear?"

"All of them," she said. "What if they're the same person? What if this person takes you next? What if… if… if…"

She wiped away a tear. Marnie felt a whole lot of guilt, but not enough to back off. She had a gut feeling about this situation and she was going to figure out who was behind everything.

I bet it's Terry Jacobson. He's all poor me around adults but all of us at school know he's a jerk.

"Mom," she said. "There will be police and search and rescue people all over the canyon. My friends are on their way right now. It sounds like most of Southern California will be up there searching for Nina, Suzie, and Barbie."

"But you're my baby," Mom wailed. "I don't want you hurt." She sniffled and wiped her eyes with a tissue. "I know you and your dad have this insatiable desire to dig into problems and get answers. Neither of you ever thinks about stopping until you've solved the problem."

"I have to do this," Marnie said. "It's like you going back to college after all these years, to become a teacher. What would you do if someone said it was too dangerous to teach? Would you quit?"

"Being a teacher isn't life-threatening," Mom said. "I can handle anything a student does. The kind of job you want is a very different situation all together. You have no idea what a cornered criminal will do."

"I'm going to college to learn that," Marnie said. "And I will take classes to protect myself. You know Dad has already been teaching me some moves."

The boldness running through Marnie pushed her to stand up for her chosen profession. She'd never argued like this with her parents when they wanted her to back off a problem in the past, but this was too personal to sit on her porch and wonder what was going on.

"I'm going with you." Mom turned to stare at Marnie. "There is no one on this earth who can stop me. I will not let anyone hurt my child."

The image of her mom tagging along petrified Marnie. She was eighteen, old enough to vote, and her mom wanted to hold her hand to make sure she didn't trip over her own feet. Shudders ran through her muscles and she found it hard to breathe.

What if Mom wants to go along on all of our cases? What can I do to stop her?

There was no time to figure out an answer to those questions or argue with her mother. Brakes squealed and a vehicle no normally seen in the area came to a stop. Garth's dad had shipped the Range Rover to California from Australia a few years back, after he spoke at a symposium on law enforcement in Sydney. Tish, Les, Garth, and Brad climbed out of Garth's Range Rover. Marnie couldn't help laughing at the sight of that vehicle. It was boxy and tall, with luggage racks on top and the spare tire fastened to the hood. His gas mileage was horrible but he loved it because he could go out in the desert and have tons of fun. She agreed with that part, having joined him on more than one Saturday in the high desert around Lancaster and Palmdale.

"What's going on?" Les pointed at Marnie's car. "Who did that?"

"The question of the day." Marnie leaned against the railing, noticing that her friends were outfitted for a day of hiking in the mountains. "Come on up and I'll fill you in."

Everyone gathered on the porch. Mom looked them over and shook her head.

"I still don't like this," she said. "But I can see that you're all determined to be part of this search."

She ran down the steps and hurried over to Dad. Marnie bit her lip, certain they were about to be kept away from the action.

"What was that all about?" Tish asked.

"Mom's upset," Marnie said. "She's scared that whoever did this will hurt me, or that I'll disappear like Suzie, Nina, and Barbie did."

"Fat chance of that happening," Garth laughed. "Whoever this is will run in fear if he tries messing with you girls. I won't mess with the three of you, after Marnie's dad taught you how to protect yourselves."

She appreciated his support but knew they were in for a lot of problems if they confronted the person behind these crimes. Marnie wasn't even sure the creeper, kidnapper, and car destroyer were the same person. It could be three different people and she was unlucky enough to be involved with all of them at once.

"We have to be careful," Marnie said. "This isn't an easy case like our others have been. We could get into real trouble out in the hills today."

"Yeah." Garth nodded. "I understand that. Brad and I have a plan. I'll go with you and he'll stick with Tish and Les."

That sounded like a great plan, one her mom couldn't argue with, not without seeming foolish. Marnie nodded and glanced at her dad.

He didn't look happy.

Chapter Thirteen

"Now what?" Marnie asked. "Dad looks like he's about to tell us to stay behind."

"He can't do that," Tish said. "The police asked us to assist them yesterday—officially."

She had a good point, one Marnie hadn't thought of while her parents were being so overprotective. They had been asked to assist yesterday. Dad might try to stop them but they had a task to accomplish, and they had to prove they were worthy of that job. What better way than helping with the search?

"You're right." Marnie grinned. "Mom won't like it but we were asked to assist."

Pulling a tan leather butterfly stick barrette out of her jeans pocket and holding it in her mouth, she twisted her waist-length hair up against her head and then with one hand, got the barrette fastened. Tish did the same with a square leather stick barrette on her hair.

Marnie felt so much better. Sure, she was a little tired and hiking around the canyon wouldn't help with that feeling but right now, she knew they had a solid chance to find their missing classmates.

Suzie's been gone for three days. She might be in bad shape. Hopefully, Barbie and Nina aren't hurt.

"Okay." Dad clapped his hands once. "Wildcat Crew, you're taking the trail off Canyon Road. Grab some whistles from the S&R Team and be ready to take off as soon as we finish a few things here."

Garth and Brad went after the whistles. Marnie kept an eye on her dad, noticing how he took command and was professional despite everything going on personally.

He waved the officers hanging around the house over to him. "Guys, great of you to volunteer for this but we need some of you on patrol. We have enough off-duty officers to cover every possible location those girls could be if one of them screamed and was heard this far out of the canyon."

The officers in uniform grumbled but all except two of them left. Those men stationed themselves on either end of the porch. Their seemingly relaxed posture told Marnie that until they discovered whoever had vandalized her car and was sneaking around the house after dark was located, she wouldn't be without a police officer close to take care of the situation.

"Jonathon," Mom said. "We need to talk."

"Marty." Dad clasped Mom's cheeks. "I know what you're feeling. I feel the exact same way right this very minute, but our little girl is growing up. She's a very good investigator, as she's proven since this whole mess started."

"But she's a girl," Mom said. "Hiking, surfing, even driving her own car is fine, but your job is dangerous."

"Any job is dangerous," he said. "You could walk into a situation in a classroom that would put you in mortal danger. Don't tell me it can't happen, my beloved Marty. The world is changing faster than we can keep up. I always hope whenever I see a terrible case that things will improve, but they don't."

Mom's real name was Martha, but she'd always gone by Marty. As a child, she'd been more of a tomboy than Marnie was.

Maybe I need to remind Mom how much she used to do stuff like this. Marnie shook her head. *No way. I don't want her getting mad.*

A van pulled up in front of the house. After the driver slanted his wheels, so they were braced against the curb, the rear doors opened and half a dozen men hopped out and put chocks against them.

"Mobile command post," Tish said. "Why are they here?"

Dad glanced at her. "They're here because we're going to be in some pretty rough terrain up there. All of you will be the closest to Canyon Road, to give you a better chance of getting out in case we need to evacuate."

"Evacuate why?" Brad asked.

The concern on his face touched Marnie in a way she wouldn't have thought was possible. Since learning that he had feelings for Suzie, Marnie saw Brad in a much different light. He was more than a brainy kid who didn't fit in. He was as normal as they were.

"Fire, son," Dad said. "It's been tinder dry this year. We're going to be tromping around in some mighty rocky ground. Whoever screamed last night might have fallen off a trail, be stuck in a gulley, the good Lord only knows what's going on up there. That means we need to bring in the command post to coordinate where everyone is and assign new search grids when they clear where they're working."

"That makes sense," Brad said, nodding. "Thanks for explaining."

Marnie nearly busted out laughing when she saw one of the people with the mobile command post pulling out boxes filled with electric percolators and everything necessary to make coffee.

"Mrs. Wildwood," the man said. "Do you mind if we set up in your kitchen? This kind of operation—"

"Runs on coffee," Mom said. "I haven't been a police officer's wife for twenty years without learning coffee is a food group for all of you." She pointed at the porch. "Come on. I'll show you where to set up."

After the man joined her on the porch, she grinned at him.

"I suppose you have sandwich makings in there too."

"Yes, ma'am," he said.

"Looks like you and I are going to be busy." She glanced at Marnie. "Don't take any chances up there. Come back in one piece."

Everyone gathered at the mobile command post. The Wildcat Crew were given whistles and a map that had squares on it.

"Ever used a grid map before?" the officer asked.

"No," Tish said and glanced at the others.

"Not me," Brad said.

"What's a grid map?" Les asked.

Marnie shook her head, although she'd heard of them from Dad.

"Sure." Garth held out his hand. "Dad and I go caving every summer in Missouri. I can explain one."

"Great." The officer handed over two maps. "You kids will take the section outlined in red. When you finish a grid, call in the information, by using the numbers printed in that area." He handed Marnie and Les portable radios. "Do you need a lesson in these?"

"No," Marnie said. "Dad taught us how to use them a few years back."

"Okay." He nodded at the rest of the search team. "Call us if you see anything out of place. That means anything that doesn't seem normal. Or if you get into trouble."

"We will," she said, planning to do just the opposite.

They took a step. Dad held up a hand.

"Did all of you put on suntan lotion?" he asked. "That sun is pretty strong today."

"Swedish Tanning Secret applied a couple of hours ago," Marnie said. "Anything else?"

"Make sure you grab some of the bottled water from the command post," he said. "And be careful out there."

"We will."

"And come back when we tell you to," he said. "No deciding to keep looking because you have a gut feeling."

"Sure."

Marnie was going to keep looking until she found Nina, Suzie, and Barbie. No one would hold her back from discovering why they had disappeared and who was responsible.

Chapter Fourteen

The Mastermind knelt behind the thick shrubs at a vacant lot across the street from the Wildwood house. He hadn't been able to get away once Marnie and her parents saw the devastation he'd done to her car.

"That last touch was a masterpiece," he whispered. "Dumb broad probably cried like a baby."

It had been too dark to gauge her reaction. Once the pigs showed up in force, he didn't dare leave his hiding place to sneak away. That was no problem for him. The satisfaction he got from everyone working on the car and planning a search of the canyon made him feel very good. He was finally getting through to these fools that he was someone to be reckoned with.

"They should have figured that out four years ago," he whispered, making certain that his voice didn't attract attention. "But nooooooo. Those damn Manson freaks had to spoil all my fun."

He wanted the shotgun he'd used on his whiny family. They were dragging him down with their rules and constantly getting on his nerves. Nothing he did was good enough for them.

"Just because Dad was the starting quarterback since he was a freshman didn't mean I was a loser because I was third string," he muttered. "I was good but the coach didn't see that. We haven't won more than a couple of games a season because of the stupid guys on defense. It's not my fault, nothing is."

A smug expression on his face, he had to hold back laughter as the pigs and those stupid kids took off into the canyon. No one would find anything. The house where he'd hidden his captives and where he'd bring the rest of those he would destroy as soon as this quieted down wasn't on any map. As far as he knew, after asking around, no one knew it existed—except him and three dumb broads. He was pretty sure Wildcat Crew would be around where he'd hidden those girls, but no one would disturb that area now. He'd made sure of that by putting a chain across the entrance with a "No Trespassing" sign on it.

"It's such a sacred place," His whisper was reverent. "So much power. Restful. I am in control there."

He'd tried to research the building but there were no records, except a back page mention in the *Monrovia News Post* about how a man claiming to be a doctor performed illegal surgeries on unwilling victims in the abandoned building during the 1940s.

"I felt the pain of those he operated on. Their terror lives in the walls," The Mastermind said. "His experiments will continue, but I will be so much better than he was. No one will catch me."

The sound of doors slamming returned his attention to the Wildwood house. No one had moved from their previous position. They were all hanging around and talking. He smiled, baring his teeth and holding back maniacal laughter.

His prisoners were safely in his hands. No one would find them.

"Time to deal with Uncle Jim."

Crawling backward, he moved with as much stealth as he could. A couple of times, he had to lie flat against the overgrown grass, hoping no one noticed that he was in the open and crushing the vegetation.

To his relief, the pigs moved into the canyon, along with those nosy kids.

Wildcat Crew, what a stupid name. They're more like misfits.

Continuing his painfully slow retreat away from potential trouble, he managed to get into a neighboring backyard. No one was home but there was one of those small dogs with an irritating bark announcing his presence. Unfortunately, it was inside the sliding glass door to what appeared to be a dining room.

"I'll come back later and take care of you." He pointed at the animal and mimicked pulling the trigger on a gun. "Believe me, I will come back."

Slipping through yards, avoiding barking dogs, and hopping over fences, he got down to Foothill Boulevard and walked a few blocks to a cul-de-sac. He ran up the hill, panting halfway up, and cut through some more yards. Thankfully, these people didn't have any loud, obnoxious pets. He was able to get to the house he revered as much as he did that one in the hills.

"That you, boy?" Uncle Jim asked as soon as he was in the door.

"Yeah." The Mastermind pulled off his grass and dirt-stained T-shirt and dropped it on the kitchen floor. "What do you want?"

"A bit of respect might be in order," Uncle Jim said. "Since you don't seem capable of that much, could you possibly explain why you weren't here when I woke up this morning?"

Clad in nothing except sneakers, shorts, and a white tank style undershirt, The Mastermind went into the living room.

"I was jogging," he said. "Have to stay in shape if I want to make first string at USC."

He'd mocked up an acceptance letter from USC in order to fool the old man into thinking he was going to a university. In truth, no one had accepted his applications. They'd all indicated that his less than stellar performance on the football field in addition to his 2.5 GPA didn't make him a good candidate for their institutions. Both USC and UCLA had suggested that he spend a couple of years at a junior college, where he wouldn't have the intense pressure a four year university put on him. They'd hinted that he could reapply after doing that and they would reconsider him for admission.

I am not going to a loser junior college. Their football teams don't get any kind of attention. Only losers go to those places.

He really wasn't interested in college anyway. His path was set. College wasn't necessary for the person destined to make Manson's followers look like amateurs.

Chapter Fifteen

Marnie climbed into the front passenger seat of the Range Rover. Brad, Tish, and Les were already in the back. As soon as Garth was seated, he buckled his seat belt and put the key in the ignition.

"Buckle up," he said. "I promised Dad that no one would ride in this vehicle without a seatbelt."

"Yeah," Marnie said. "I remember."

She fastened her belt and glanced at the others. Marnie wanted to see their expressions once he got this beast moving. To say that Garth was still getting used to the four-wheel drive vehicle with a stick shift was an understatement. Since he'd parked on an uphill, she held on tight to the door handle.

"I'm not that bad," he protested.

"I remember our last trip into the desert," she said. "Hang on, everyone. This might get bumpy."

She smiled at the memory. She and Garth and spent an afternoon photographing the wildflowers around Palmdale and Lancaster earlier in the year. There had been a short rain shower not long before they called it a day and he hadn't taken that possibility into consideration when parking on the side of the road. When they got back to the Range Rover, it had been tilting dangerously to one side—the passenger side. She'd had to crawl into the seat where she was now through the driver's door and had strapped in as soon as she felt balanced. He'd rocked the vehicle back and forth several times, causing her to grimace and stare at how close she was to the desert floor before he finally managed to get them back on the road and heading home.

"There's no sand around." Garth started the engine, put the vehicle into gear, and jerked. "Aw, nuts," he said when the engine died. "Forgot I was on a hill."

Everyone was laughing when he finally got away from the curb. Marnie held onto hope that they would find their classmates.

Fifteen minutes later, Garth parked in front of a chained entrance with a "No Trespassing" sign on it. Marnie stared at it in dismay.

"When did that go up?" she asked. "I don't remember this being here."

The others joined her.

"What's up?" Tish asked. "There's nothing up that track."

"Weird." Brad scratched his head. "Maybe someone bought the property."

The others concurred with him. Garth pointed across the track.

"We'll start on this side," he said.

"Yeah." Marine handed Brad the grid map. "How about a refresher course on using one of these."

"Easy." Garth pointed at the path they were standing on and then at the area directly across from them. "This is the edge of two grids. Brad, Tish, and Les will go east. You and I go west, Marnie. We use an estimation to make sure we search each grid."

"What do we use to estimate when we get to the other end?" Les asked.

"The normal human foot, heel to toe, about thirty steps," he said and grinned. "I think."

"Or." Marnie pointed at survey stakes driven into the ground. "What about using those?"

"Well, if you want to do it the easy way, that's fine by me."

Laughing, they all took off to start their search.

***

Five hours later, Garth had Marnie call in their last grid as clear and they headed toward his Range Rover. She had a sense that they had missed something very important, yet couldn't figure out what. He was teasing her about taking this too seriously.

"Really? Did you really just say that?" She stopped, slammed her fists against her hips, and glared at him. "Are you kidding me?"

"Yeah." He shook his head. "Bad joke."

They crossed over to where his vehicle was. Garth unlocked and opened the doors, so they could let out some of the heat. Marnie handed him a water bottle and took one for herself.

She lifted the bottle and drank deeply, taking in the heavy brush around two posts. Her dad was right about it being dry this year. Her gaze moved from left to right. Marnie was bothered deeply by this particular track being blocked. Unless she'd heard wrong, everything in the canyon belonged to the state or county. No one from those organizations would block a road that might be needed if a brush fire began. For all she knew, this was simply a fire road leading nowhere.

That's probably what it is. I've been worrying about something up there for nothing.

Yet, the posts and fence made no sense if it was a fire road. Responses in that situation didn't give the firefighters or forest rangers any time to get out of their vehicle and take down a chain or unlock a gate. Fire roads were never blocked.

"Seen the others yet?" he asked.

"No, but I can hear them shouting," she said.

It was weird. Dad had mentioned how sounds could get turned around up here in the canyon. She'd experienced it herself on several occasions, but never in the way it was happening today.

"Marnie." Garth stared at her. "That's not our group."

She turned around and stared at the chain with the "No Trespassing" sign on it. "Do you—"

Her question was interrupted by a very loud and terrorized scream.

Chapter Sixteen

Marnie scrambled to pull the radio from her rear pocket, where she'd stuffed it after calling in the last time. Garth raced around the Range Rover and yanked on the chain.

"It's not coming loose," he shouted.

"Okay, be there in a second," she said. "Did they give us a call sign?"

"I don't remember."

She fumbled with the portable radio until she turned it on. Pressing down on the switch, after listening to see if anyone else was broadcasting, she took and released a deep breath.

"This is Marnie," she said. "We're at a path with a 'No Trespassing' sign on it. We just heard a scream down that track. Les, Tish, Brad, do you read?"

"This is mobile command post, Marnie," an officer said. "Stay on the road. We're getting the team closest to you on the move now."

"Not happening." She glanced at Garth.

He was still struggling with the chain.

"We're here," Brad shouted.

She jerked her head around and saw him with Les and Tish running toward her and Garth.

"Jump it," she yelled. "Come on, guys. Down here."

Tossing the radio onto the seat of the Range Rover through the still open door, she ran over to Garth.

"Forget that. Go around."

The rest of their team got up to the chain as she and Garth were moving around it.

"Brad, stay here," Marnie shouted. "If someone shows up from the command post, let them know where we went."

"Where's the radio?" Brad yelled.

"In my Range Rover," Garth said with a laugh. "Give us some time to get down this track before you turn it back on."

"Why?" Tish ran up to them with Les on her heels.

"They told us to stay up here," Marnie said.

"Not happening," Les said.

Everyone was on the other side of the chain, except Brad, in seconds. Marnie took one last glance back at him, noticing his forlorn expression.

"Make them let you show them the way when they get here," she called. "That way you can lead them."

"Sure will." Brad waved and grinned.

The midday sun beat down on them as they trudged along the road. Every emotion Marnie possessed urged her to run but she knew better. They hadn't brought along water, or a first aid kit, in case it was needed.

"Damn." She glanced back at Brad but he was out of sight. "Where did he go?"

"We just went over a rise," Les said. "How far?"

"Not sure," Garth said. "The scream was loud but you know how sound carries out here."

"It's hot." Tish shaded her eyes and stared across the distance. "Is there a building up here?"

"Not that I've heard of," Marnie said. "I didn't even know this path had a chain blocking access."

She thought about that. The chain wasn't old but it wasn't new either. The sign wasn't an official one put in place by the police, just a piece of metal with the words spray painted on it.

Could someone have put that up to keep people out? But out of what? I've never heard of anything up here. Even Dad said there was nothing up here and he's hiked this canyon from one end to the other a bunch of times.

She could hear the faint sound of sirens approaching in the distance and picked up the pace. The others followed her lead.

A few minutes later, they all stopped abruptly.

"What is that?" Garth asked.

Before them stood a crumbling house that was probably magnificent once upon a time. Before she went back to college, Mom had been interested in old homes in the area. Marnie had enjoyed going around with her, looking at the restored places up against the foothills.

The house they were standing in front of could only be described as about to fall over in a good wind.

The shreds of lace curtains fluttered in the cracked or shattered windows. Very little paint remained on the wooden exterior to indicate what color it had once been, unless sun and wind-beaten gray was an actual paint color. As far as she could see, the stairs didn't exist any longer. A domed entrance area had four massive columns in what looked like some kind of stone holding up the roof. A splintered railing could be seen on the ground.

The wind blew up dust around them and brought a sense of evil, of horror unchecked. Marnie shivered.

"Spooky," Tish said. "What is this place? Why haven't we heard of it?"

Marnie wracked her brain for any type of legend or story that she'd heard that might explain this building.

A glimmer of a memory returned. She kept on thinking, trying to flesh out the information she'd read in the *Monrovia News Post*.

"I think." She glanced at the others. "Maybe about five years ago, there was an article in the newspaper about a place where..."

"...a doctor performed illegal surgeries," Garth said. "I remember that." He pointed at the house. "Is this the place?"

"Not sure," she said.

Marnie knew they were stalling about going inside.

"*Help us! Please! He's going to kill us!*"

Any thought of stalling vanished. She raced toward the side of the front porch, slapped the rotting wood with her hands and vaulted upward. Landing on her knees, she scrambled to her feet and ran for the door.

"Right behind you," Garth called.

The others shouted out that they were following him. She didn't pay any attention to them. The door didn't cause her much of a problem getting through it. A well-placed kick knocked it off the hinges. Marnie raced inside and quickly took in her surroundings.

She was in a shadowed hallway with other hallways leading off into the house.

"Where are you?" she called.

"Down here! Basement!"

That sounded like Barbie. Marnie raced toward the center hallway and skidded to a stop when she saw a door inset into the wall. Grabbing the knob, she turned it.

It didn't budge.

"Let me." Garth shoved past her and grabbed the knob with both hands. "Step back. Not sure how this thing opens."

He placed one foot on the wall, turned the knob with both hands, and leaned backward. The door lurched toward him and then flew open. Garth fell on the floor. Marnie rushed past him and peered into the gloom below here.

"Are you down here?" she shouted.

"Yes. We're down here."

"That's Nina!" Tish shouted. "I'll run back and tell Brad to notify the police to call for an ambulance."

"Wait!" Marnie held up a hand. "You've had a first aid course. The rest of us haven't. Les, you go to Brad."

"On my way," Les said and took off.

Marnie walked carefully down the stairs, testing each one as she moved. She wanted to run but was afraid of one of the steps breaking and her falling to the floor below. She could hear Garth and Tish coming behind her; they were also moving slowly.

"Do you see them yet?" Tish asked.

"I can't see anything," Marnie said.

She could hear soft sobbing though. Fury ran through her. Nobody deserved this kind of treatment.

Her foot finally touched the floor, which was dirt. She looked in all directions but couldn't tell where the missing girls were.

"Can you tell me where you are?" she asked.

"Not really." Barbie hiccupped. "Near a window."

"That's a lot of help." Marnie moved forward with a hand held out. She touched a wall and walked along it until she saw light coming through a window.

"Hurry," Nina said, hiccupping. "He said he'd be back for us."

Turning a corner, Marnie stopped and clapped a hand over her mouth.

"What?" Tish bumped into her. "Oh no!"

"What's going on?" Garth asked.

"They're tied to posts," Marnie said, her voice cracking with the horrified emotions running through her. "It looks like Suzie is unconscious."

She hoped Suzie was unconscious. Marnie didn't want to have discovered a body.

Chapter Seventeen

"Tish, help Barbie," Garth said, shoving past them. "Take care of Nina, Marnie."

He reached into his pocket, pulling out a pocketknife, and proceeded to cut the captives free of their ropes. Marnie caught Nina as she stood and swayed from side to side. Tish grabbed Barbie and slung one of her arms around her neck. Marnie did the same with Nina.

Garth lifted Suzie into his arms.

"You guys follow me," he said. "Wait until I get to the top of the stairs. Stay clear of the bottom."

He took off quickly. Marnie understood what he was telling them. Garth didn't want them directly behind him in case he fell on the stairs. She wasn't very happy about that and thought she should have gone up first, to help him at the top, but admired him for thinking of their safety.

"Don't fall," Tish whispered. "Please don't fall."

"Stay safe," Marnie said in a quiet voice. "Don't get hurt."

They watched him walk up the stairs, step-by-step, with Suzie draped over his shoulder. Marnie held her breath when he reached the top and swayed from side to side before catching his balance.

"Coast is clear," Garth said and stepped to one side. "Hurry. We don't know when that person is coming back."

"Go first," Marnie said to Tish. "You can help Garth with Suzie while I come up."

"Okay," Tish said. "See you upstairs."

Marnie watched her assisting Barbie up the stairs. Barbie was a mess, sobbing and tripping. Marnie worried that a step would break, but they made it to the top safely.

"Come on," Tish called after walking out of sight. "Everything is good up here."

"We're starting up now," Marnie called.

She guided Nina to the steps.

"Take your time," Marnie said. "I'll be right behind you. Just remember to test the steps before you put your foot down fully."

"Okay." Nina hiccupped again. "How did you know we were here?"

"Luck."

Marnie couldn't think of any other explanation. Her mom had wanted to stop them, but failed when Dad pointed out how important it was for her to follow her dreams. The person in charge of the search gave them what he thought was the safest assignment and they ended going in another direction, because they were close enough to hear a scream. Everything added up to a massive dose of luck in her opinion.

The trip up seemed to take forever. She could hear Nina breathing hard and noticed a huge bump on the back of her head. Marnie also heard Garth and Tish speaking in low voices about Suzie. Barbie was sobbing softly near the door.

I really want the creep who did this to come after me. Boy is he in for a surprise.

"Do you know who did this?" she asked.

"We never saw him," Nina said. "We were up here... we were messing around and then someone smacked me. That's all I remember."

They crept slowly up the stairs. A couple of times, Marnie stopped Nina from moving, until she felt the step to make sure it wasn't about to fall apart.

The sense of evil, of unrelenting horror was still with Marnie. She couldn't wait to get outside, into the sunshine. Once she saw her dad, she would ask him if there was a way to get rid of this house forever. Not only was it a terrible place to be in but it was a death trap to anyone who might discover it.

They'd finally all made it to the top of the stairs. Garth was lifting Suzie and Tish was assisting Barbie to her feet.

"I can't do anything for Suzie," Tish said. "Whatever is wrong with her is way beyond first aid. I think she's dehydrated but I can't be sure."

Marnie silently scolded herself for not thinking to bring some bottles of water with them. That might have helped now.

"Let's go," Garth said. "Marnie, you first with Nina, then Tish and Barbie. I'll need your help getting Suzie off the porch."

***

The Mastermind strolled toward his hiding place. He'd had to use another way up into the canyon, to avoid the pigs swarming all over it. It had taken him more time than usual but he wasn't worried about his captives. They weren't going to die today. And he'd brought water along to be sure they didn't die of thirst.

Nobody dies until I decide they do.

He could hear voices but was sure they weren't where he was headed. The Mastermind had heard voices since getting outside the city, mostly from the pigs yelling out "clear" all the time. His grin widened. Everyone was running around because of him.

I love this. Nobody knows who I am but they're giving me so much satisfaction.

Coming around a bend in the road, he stared at the house in horror. There were people coming out the front door. And those people—*Damn, that's Marnie and her Wildcat Crew*—they had *his* captives!

He dropped the water and snuck into the brush, remaining hidden. His only task now was to find a way to get those stupid girls back into the basement. And capture the four nosy brats who'd found them.

Success! I'll have seven in my special place, even if I have to wait for a few minutes. He thought about the symmetry of the number seven. *I only need one more for my plan to succeed! Les will be back soon from wherever she is. That will make exactly the right amount captives!* The Mastermind grinned. *Nobody can stop me now. I will be feared by the world!*

His current task was more important than making sure Suzie, Nina, and Barbie got a drink.

***

All of them moved as fast as possible and were soon out in the sunshine. Marnie and Tish assisted Nina and Barbie off the porch. Marnie returned and held out her arms.

"Lower Suzie to me," she said. "I'm balanced."

"Be careful." Garth lowered Suzie into her arms. "Wait for me to take her back. She's a little too heavy for you to carry back to the Range Rover."

He jumped down and came over to her. Marnie became aware of the sound of sirens approaching their location. She let Garth take Suzie back and turned around.

Marnie stared at the house. Her nerves were jumpy, the same way they were the night the creeper showed up.

"Guys." She faced her friends and gasped.

Terry rose from behind some thick brush. He pointed at her. That didn't scare her as much as the crazed look on his face.

"Damn bitch!"

"What are you doing?" Tish screamed.

Terry charged toward them. He was carrying a huge knife in his hands. Without thinking, Marnie dropped down into a crouch, threw her left leg out, and swung it.

"Arrrrrrgh!" Terry screamed, falling backward and landing in an awkward sprawl. Tish and Marnie sat on him to keep him down.

The knife flew out of his hands and landed several feet away. Marnie didn't worry that Terry could get to it. He was too busy squirming and trying to get free—something that wouldn't happen.

The sound of the sirens continued to get closer and closer. Marnie and the others faced the track up to the house and saw the police heading toward them at a dead run.

Chapter Eighteen

The only thing Marnie felt was relief. Her dad picked up the knife while other officers handcuffed Terry and dragged him over to one of the patrol cars. Paramedics jumped out of their vehicle and ran over to where Garth was holding Suzie, taking her from him.

"I should scold you until you can't hear," Dad said. "What possessed you to come up here?"

"We heard a scream," Marnie said. "Come on, Dad. What did you tell Mom earlier?"

She held back on telling him to take his own advice, but only because of the woman getting out of the last police car to arrive. She looked a lot like Suzie, but was tall and slender.

"Suzie!" the new arrival screamed. "Is she okay?"

"Is that Christine?" Marnie asked.

"Yes," Dad said. "Okay, I understand why you did this, but please don't try this stunt again. That was a very dangerous man you confronted."

She smiled, thinking of the conversation they were going to have later, when she would ask him to teach her a few more defensive moves.

***

A few hours later, Marnie and her friends walked through the emergency entrance of Arcadia Methodist Hospital. They had to wade through reporters from what looked like every news organization in the Los Angeles area. Since LA was a West Coast hub for news, there were also reporters from the national headquarters in New York.

"There they are!" someone shouted. "Those kids stopped 'The Mastermind.'"

"Huh?" Garth scratched his head. "Who is that idiot talking about?"

"Terry Jacobson," Dad said. "He shouted that he was 'The Mastermind' when we got him to the police station. Unfortunately, the news groups had people there too. Reporters are lapping up this story. I really hope they don't make that young man as infamous as the Manson Family."

The Mastermind. Marnie couldn't help giggling. *Terry really thought he was some kind of mastermind? Is he trying to say he was nuts when he did this stuff? Good grief! He'll probably have an insanity defense.*

Since meeting Dad here, she and the others had learned that Terry had babbled out his whole plan for the summer solstice along with confessing to murdering his family. He'd also laughed about seriously injuring his uncle. Marnie was pretty sure he would attempt an insanity defense. His actions guaranteed a life without parole sentence if he didn't.

"Please, you have to tell me about my sister. Her name is Suzie Ad... Calderone."

Marnie stared at the woman. She was pretty, even when worried. It was freaky how much she looked like Suzie.

"There's Christine," Dad said. "I want the five of you to talk to her. We still have to find George. Christine said she wasn't sure of where he was but I suspect otherwise."

"Why?" Les asked.

"She kept shifting her eyes around the room," he said. "She wouldn't look at me when she was responding to my questions."

"Is there any chance she knows where her parents are?" Tish asked.

"No," Dad said. "She thinks they might have gone to Mexico but doesn't know where. Christine remembers some unspecified threats to move there if the kids ever brought the notice of the police onto them and their activities."

"Anything else you need to know, Detective Wildwood?" Garth asked.

"Not at the moment," Dad said. "I'll take the press outside and talk to them. That way, people who need to get in here won't have to fight their way through them."

He walked away, through the crowd of reporters. Their questions began immediately, but Dad kept moving until he was outside.

"Les, you're with me," Marnie said. "We'll talk to Christine. Garth, you and Tish see what you can find out about Barbie and Nina. Don't let them leave until we talk to them."

"What about me?" Brad asked.

"Stay with Les and me," Marnie said. "Maybe Christine knowing how you feel about Suzie will help her open up with us."

"How did you—" His face flushed scarlet. "I didn't think anyone realized that I loved Suzie."

The team split up. Marnie waited until Garth and Tish were in the emergency room before heading over to where Christine was leaning against the admittance desk and talking to a nurse.

"You don't understand," Christine said. "She is my sister. Her real name is Adams, but our parents... Ah, never mind. I'll find an officer to explain the whole mess."

She turned away, almost bumping into Marnie. Christine was crying, silent tears that usually indicated a person was very upset.

"Hi. Marnie Wildwood." Marnie held out her hand. "This is Les Johnson and Brad Montgomery. Can you sit and talk to us? Please? We need some information on your brother."

"Why?" Christine eyed them suspiciously. "Are you going to get Detective Wildwood to arrest George? He didn't do anything except get involved with Beverly Hills Police Department as a snitch."

This was news to Marnie. She thought her dad would have told them everything, unless he didn't know about BHPD using George as an informant.

"Dad didn't tell me George was helping the police." Marnie guided her group over to a group of empty chairs far from everyone else in the waiting room. "Did you tell him about that?"

"No." Christine shook her head. "George told me the night he disappeared."

"Want to tell us about it?" Les asked. "You might remember something you didn't tell Detective Wildwood."

"It's worth a shot." Christine shrugged her shoulders. "Really can't hurt and I would like to know what happened to George." She glanced at the emergency room doors. "Talking to you is better than trying to get information out of these people."

Marnie could understand her anger. It was hard to wait for information when an investigation was going on, as she'd learned during this case.

"Our parents weren't the usual kind of parents," Christine said. "They worked from home. All of us thought that was normal, until we got close to being teenagers."

Marnie leaned forward, drinking in every word. Christine explained how she and George discovered the marijuana growing not far from their backyard. They'd attempted to destroy the fledgling plants, that year's first crop, by taking hoes to them. They'd been caught by the family gardener and reported to their parents, who had retaliated by grounding them from any activity other than attending school for a month. That was when George took some of the marijuana hidden in a storage unit. He'd been planning to turn it in to the police department, but someone at school had seen him and phoned in a report.

"Things got worse after that," Christine said. "Our parents wouldn't even let us go to the bathroom without watching us. They searched our rooms, backpacks, even our bodies daily, so we wouldn't attempt to ruin their business again. George finally called a detective at Beverly Hills Police Department and was going there the next day to explain everything. That night, our parents and some guys dressed in white slacks, shirts, and shoes took George for a ride. He threw me a desperate look but couldn't say anything. They'd gagged him." She wiped away a tear. "Then he was gone. I knew I was next. Our parents were watching me too closely for my comfort. I went to school one morning and snuck off campus at lunch. A friend of mine who'd graduated the previous year was waiting for me. She brought me to Monrovia and paid for my apartment for six months. Luckily, I was able to get a job and a car before the end of that period."

Liz leaned forward in her chair. "Did you try to get your sister out of that mess?"

"Yes." Christine nodded. "But they were gone—my parents and Suzie. The police were at the house, searching it. I didn't stick around to find out what they were doing, just ran back home to my apartment."

"So, you didn't know Suzie was in Monrovia?" Garth asked.

"Not until Detective Wildwood came to my apartment," Christine said. "Is there any way I can find out how my sister is?"

"I'll take care of that," Marnie said, rising. "Stay here, so the reporters don't come after you. I'm going to find Dad."

She walked away, lost in thought. Marnie could tell that Christine had been telling the truth. Her story didn't make much sense though, at least the way Marnie had been raised. Parents were loving and good, always there for their children. Yet, it seemed she'd run into one of those ugly situations her dad had warned her about far too many times.

How do we figure out where George is? Men in white shirts, pants, and shoes sounds really weird.

She looked around the Emergency Room admitting area. Dad was walking through the sliding doors at the ambulance entrance. Marnie waited for him.

"Did you get Christine to trust you?" he asked.

"I did." She explained what she'd heard. "Who wears those kinds of clothes?

I've never heard of anyone wanting to wear all white. It would get dirty."

Dad smiled. "You just discovered an important clue, Marnie. Given what George was trying to do and his age at the time, I know exactly where to start looking for him."

He whistled and turned toward the doors. Marnie stared at him.

"Aren't you going to tell me where you think he is?"

"Not until I find out if I'm right or wrong."

Shaking her head, she walked back toward her friends. By the time she got there, a doctor was talking to Christine.

"Suzie will be fine, Miss Adams," the doctor said. "She'll need to stay here for a couple of days, just so that we can make sure there isn't something we missed, but she will be able to leave with you on Monday afternoon."

"What about Nina and Barbie?" Les asked.

"They'll be going home in the morning with their parents," the doctor said. "They had bumps, bruises, and a pretty big scare, nothing worse for them."

Marnie was relieved. She also thought she'd figured out who would wear white pants, shirt, and shoes. The doctor was wearing that type of outfit.

Time to put our investigative skills to use. We need to figure out what kind of hospital George was taken to.

Chapter Nineteen

Four days after the rescue, Marnie, Les, Tish, Garth, and Brad were getting into position with the rest of their classmates. In another fifteen minutes, they would march onto the football field and get their diplomas. All of them were very excited but also a little scared about what their futures held.

"Ready for tonight?" she asked her friends.

"Totally," Garth said. "I can't wait to check out everything, especially the Haunted House. That's a wild ride."

Marnie shivered. Dad had promised to take her on that ride the day it opened. They'd had a ton of fun that afternoon but when they came home, horror intruded. He'd been informed about the murders in Beverly Hills in what would later become the Manson Family case.

"I think It's A Small World will be fun," she said. "Don't you love singing along on that ride?"

Everyone nodded and agreed. Other rides were discussed: the Matterhorn Bobsleds, Pirates of the Caribbean, Fantasyland Autopia, and Country Bear

Jamboree were added to their list of must do rides.

"What if we grab something to eat at Skull Rock and Pirate's Cove?" Les asked. "It's cool in there."

"Absolutely," Tish said.

Brad and Suzie nodded their heads in agreement.

The sounds of *Pomp and Circumstance* filled the air. They got into line and walked into the football stadium for the last time as students at Monrovia High School.

***

A few hours later, they were all back at the high school. The huge yellow buses were lined up in front at the curb. They managed to get seats together. Marnie sat sideways, with her back against a window, drinking in all the excitement around her. She was happy and scared at the same time.

"All night!" Barbie squealed. "I've never been up all night before."

"Well, don't flake out on us," a guy shouted from the back of the bus. "Bet I can do better rowing a canoe than you can."

Marnie smiled. He would learn once they arrived at the canoe ride that it closed at dark. Barbie shook her head and turned to them as the bus got on the freeway to head south.

"Thanks so much for what you did," she said. "I was so afraid that we'd never get out of that creepy house."

"Just glad you're okay," Marnie said. "What's next for you?"

"USC," Barbie said. "I'm going to nursing school. You?"

"Citrus Community College," Marnie said. "Wildcat Crew is taking courses in law enforcement there. Once we finish, we'll decide if we'll be private investigators or join the police force."

"That is so cool," Barbie said. "Good luck."

Their arrival at the massive theme park was very overwhelming. It was Graduation Night for schools all over the Los Angeles and Orange County area. Marnie stared in awe at the number of teens making their way to the gate.

Instead of the ticket book they normally would have used to access the rides, they all wore a lanyard with a placard on it, indicating they were guests of the park for the party. No one else would be inside, except chaperones and employees.

"Ready?" Tish asked once they were through the gates."

"More than ready," Brad said. "Where to first?"

"Autopia," Suzie said. "I've always wanted to try that."

Holding hands, they ran toward Fantasyland. Marnie was smiling and laughing.

***

They finished out their night with non-alcoholic mint juleps and apple fritters at the Carnation Plaza. All of them were exhausted and ready to head home. Marnie watched the sun rising in the east and was more than ready for the next mystery that would cross their path.

Wonder what it will be?

They already had plans to search for George Adams, but had to wait on her dad to discover exactly where Suzie's brother was. Marnie hoped it wouldn't take too long to get that information.

"Beach for the summer solstice?" Les asked after they'd settled on the bus for the ride home.

"Sounds like a plan," Marnie said.

She watched out the window as another beautiful Southern California day began.

About K.C. Sprayberry

"I have a secret… a very special secret. Perhaps you've heard this one before… from the time I was a child, I wanted to write stories for people to read. " *K.C. Sprayberry*

Former California native, K.C. Sprayberry traveled the U.S. and Europe before finally settling in the mountains of Northwest Georgia. She's been married to her soulmate for more than a quarter of a century and they enjoy spoiling their grandchildren along with many other activities.

Inspiration strikes at the weirdest times and drives her to grab notebook and pen to jot down her ideas. Those close to her swear nothing or no one is safe if she's smiling gently in a corner and watching those in the same room interact. Her observations have often given her ideas for her next story, set not only in the South but wherever the characters demand they settle.

Social Media

Facebook:

https://www.facebook.com/pg/AuthorKCSprayberry/

Twitter:
https://twitter.com/kcsowriter

Blog:
http://outofcontrolcharacters.blogspot.com/

Spotify:
https://open.spotify.com/collection/playlists

Goodreads:
http://www.goodreads.com/author/show/5011219.K_C_Sprayberry

Amazon Author Page:
http://www.amazon.com/-/e/B005DI1YOU

Pinterest:
http://pinterest.com/kcsprayberry/boards/

AUTHORSdB:
http://authorsdb.com/authors-directory/5230-k-c-sprayberry

MeWe:
https://mewe.com/join/kcsprayberryauthor

Website:
http://www.authorkcsprayberry.com/

YouTube:
https://www.youtube.com/channel/UCGGH
aiNhvTSsb6bXddR59iw

Authorgraph:
https://www.authorgraph.com/authors/kcso
writer

Email:
kcspray01@gmail.com

If you enjoyed this story, check out these other Solstice Publishing books by K.C. Sprayberry:

Puff of Smoke

Multi-billionaire Mark Jannson has everything money can buy. If it has no financial value, he wants nothing to do with it. International best selling romance author Sheila Carson lives only for her child, Lanie. Ben Mason fell for the lovely yet reclusive Sheila when she divorced her husband and vows to help her find her child. Eleanor Jannson has questions her dad won't answer.

An arson to cover up murder and kidnapping in Colorado's Front Range near Denver begins with a puff of smoke. For almost eleven years, Sheila never gives up hope that she will find her daughter alive, even though officially the child was declared dead in the fire that consumed her ex-husband's home. Mark lives in constant fear that his former wife will uncover his horrific secret and will do anything, including ordering another murder, to cover his tracks. Ben Mason has connections he's loathe to disclose but uses them to assist Sheila in this international murder mystery.

https://www.amazon.com/dp/B0742GJ2ZG/

The Car

For nearly a hundred years, no one knew the truth.

Mark Jameson and Belinda Sue Marsters refuse to be separated, despite how much their parents hated each other. In a bold move, they grab the opportunity to leave. What consequences will they face?

https://www.amazon.com/dp/B07FCPTRXR/

The Case of the Vanishing Girls Wildcat Crew Book 1

Finally moving on from the horror of the Manson killings, the Los Angeles area has begun to return to normal. Until, that is, the small bedroom community of Monrovia skyrockets into the news. This sleepy little area, nestled up against the foothills, is probably best known for their football team, but that was yesterday's news.

Three girls have vanished. Notes left behind have an "H" and a "S" with red dripping off them. People's minds automatically go to the horror of 1969 and wonder if someone else is about to initiate "Helter Skelter."

A group of teens, Wildcat Crew, doesn't think so. Despite the police looking at a trouble teen, they focus on another teen whose past has some dark secrets. As the city moves toward the summer solstice, these intrepid investigators work diligently on solving this case before someone else vanishes into the canyon.

https://www.amazon.com/dp/B06XPKSJKK/

The Case of the Scared Child Wildcat Crew Book 2

The summer solstice has arrived. Being the sun worshipers they are, Wildcat Crew heads to the beach for a day of fun and a picnic. But first, Marnie gets a huge surprise. Her parents have replaced her Camaro, destroyed in their first case.

At the beach with thousands of other Southern Californians, the crew stumbles over a small, crying child. Instead of checking out the waves and working on their tans, they go on the hunt for the little boy's parents.

https://www.amazon.com/dp/B0722P7Z89/

The Case of the Missing Brother Wildcat Crew Book 3

George Adams, brother to Christine and Suzie, disappeared when his parents took him out of their home in Beverly Hills. Wildcat Crew finally has the clues they need to discover where he is and why he's there.

The crew works hard but runs into all sorts of brick walls. Until they uncover important clues and are soon on their way to the successful conclusion of another case.

https://www.amazon.com/dp/B07BMZ2FV L/

The Case of Where is Marnie Wildwood? Wildcat Crew Book 4

Marnie Wildwood solves mysteries. Her friends are at her side while she seeks answers, assisting her every step of the way.

Until… vengeance comes for her "nosy" behavior. In terror packed moments, Marnie is kidnapped. Garth, Tish, Les, Suzie, and Brad desperately want to be part of the many police officers searching for the daughter of one of their own. They are told to stand down and let the professionals do the job. They have to look on and remain together under supervision while Marnie is taken far from them.

Minutes turn into hours, hours into one day followed by a second day without Marnie Wildwood being seen. She has vanished without a trace, along with her distinctive 1967 Ford Mustang.

Who can Wildcat Crew trust? Who can they depend on to help locate their leader? Where is Marnie?

Wildcat Crew takes on their toughest case. Time is running out to find Marnie. Can they accomplish the impossible?

https://www.amazon.com/dp/B07NLFWZTX

www.ingramcontent.com/pod-product-compliance
Lightning Source LLC
Chambersburg PA
CBHW070039030726
47506CB00003B/802